VENUS IN PARIS

VENUS IN PARIS

Anonymous

HEADLINE

British Library Cataloguing in Publication Data

Anonymous
Venus in Paris.
I. Title
823'.914 [F]

ISBN 0-7472-0125-0

Printed and bound in Great Britain by
Richard Clay Ltd, Bungay, Suffolk

HEADLINE BOOK PUBLISHING PLC
Headline House
79 Great Titchfield Street
London W1P 7FN

VENUS IN PARIS

CHAPTER ONE

Two women were sitting in the huge living room of one of those enormous mansions, a half-palace, with which the environs of Paris are so richly endowed. Occasionally they exchanged a few words. They were occupied with needlepoint, that seemingly endless task which was about as exciting and never ending as the many love stories which are spun out in the newspapers of Paris.

One was a beautiful brunette, about twenty-five years old, with a marvelous, soft complexion, dark, sparkling eyes and full, red lips which betrayed the sensual nature of their charming owner.

The other one, a blonde, seemed to be around twenty years old. Her face was like that of an angel, framed by golden hair. Her slender body, her hazel eyes, and the innocent smile completed the picture of perfect innocence. It was the sort of innocence that drives men wild and makes them contemplate deeds of which their bodies are not always capable.

That was one of the reasons why the innocent looking blonde, despite her tender years, wore the black dress of widowhood.

George Vaudrez had died in the attempt of giving his beloved son and heir a little playmate. Though he had not succeeded, he had died happily.

That night—now almost a year ago— George's hand had searched for his young wife's body. She had responded perfectly, opened her thighs wide, and George had crawled right on top of her, deciding to dispense with the usual preliminaries. His whole frame was flushed with a pink heat. His prick had felt bloated, aching and growing to an ecstatic bursting point. His thighs and back ached with the downward pressure, and Florentine's bobbing crotch drove him into an even wilder frenzy. The drumming in George's ears—and he had been suffering from this condition lately—became almost unbearable. He tried desperately to force the explosion out his prick before there was going to be one in his head or his chest.

His breathing had become a pitiful consumptive whine but his wife, in a state of continual spasms, showed no mercy for his tortured, pathetic state. George opened his watery eyes. In his aching head he suddenly felt the power of great emotion. His wife was so young, so passionate and so beautiful. He wanted to get her with child. Just one more.

"Oh, dear God," he thought, "one more baby that bears my name."

He wanted to hold her tight, but he no longer had the strength. He closed his eyes again and mechanically continued to push up and down. His prick seemed to be swelling larger and larger, more so than it had ever done in the past year. It seemed that it might never come out again. He writhed his loins against her, and sweat dripped from every pore of his body. The desire to come was intolerable and yet he couldn't quite seem to manage it. It would happen, he knew, but his head felt as if it was splitting and his chest was constricted. He fervently prayed that it would hurry.

Feebly he tensed his buttocks, felt a twinge of cramp and relaxed them again. He pressed his abdomen against hers, opened his eyes

10

again and fixed her with a pleading gaze. Florentine understood. Without loosing connection, she rolled over and George was now on his back, with Florentine riding him! She sensed from his writhing and his agonized gasps and groans that he was about to come. This unexpected situation, plus her new sense of mastery of the situation, made her unleash her body and she began to pummel him for all she was worth. She let herself be carried away by her own momentous passion.

She could feel her loins swarming as if a thousand snakes were writhing inside. She had not felt this way since that night, a long time ago, when she was stranded with Gordon, the young Duke of Herisey in the little village of Bretoncelles.

Florentine released a stream of gasping cries which broke through the blackness in George's head and revived him in a last flush of passion so that he thrust his loins up at her, mumbled painfully through dry lips, groaned agonizingly and clenched his fingers into her thighs with a last strength.

Dazedly he opened his eyes again. His loins seemed to be covered with a sticky wetness amidst Florentine's moanings. His prick felt grazed, beaten, full of something that had to escape. He saw her head mistily, head thrown back, hair flowing about her shoulders. Her face was contorted, her lips curled, showing her pearly white teeth. His fingers dug hard into her fleshy thighs, then groped for the curly fleece which was keeping his member a prisoner of agonizing pleasure. The climax was near . . . it was on him . . . there! He gasped deliriously, and felt his organ explode as if in a

11

hundred pieces. George fought for breath, fought for consciousness, but felt himself losing both. He tried to appeal to her, but she was riding him in total frenzy, riding him till she had reached her own, explosive climax. George slowly slipped off into a painful darkness.

Florentine had echoed her husband's feelings with precision. The moment he dropped off in relaxation, her own climax spasmed through her body. Her flood of sensation swamped up in her crotch with a dragging, delightful agony. Just at that moment his prick had seemed to be at its biggest in her, so that she felt it would smash right through her and up into her belly.

For some seconds afterward, still excited and hardly knowing that she had come, she had swayed about on his prostrate body and then she had flopped down on top of him. It took her almost five minutes to collect her wits.

The first thing she realized was that George Vaudrez was not just lying still through exhaustion. She tried to kiss him, but his lips were turning cold. She lifted an eyelid and death stared at her. With a terrifying scream the young wife leaped off the bed. A servant was dispatched to call the doctor. He could do nothing but declare that his good friend had died happily.

Her sister, the brunette, Donna Julia de Corriero, also wore mourning. She, too, had become a widow at very young age, though in not as stormy a manner as her unfortunate, younger sister. Her honor and reputation had been saved by an old friend, the General Don José, who in his dotage had offered his hand, heart and fortune to Julia. The girl had gratefully accepted because Count Gaston Saski, whose mistress she had been, had jilted her upon the orders of his aunt who held the purse strings in the family. Don José had treated her like a beloved daughter, and not once had his thoughts strayed to the possibilities of carnal pleasures with the luscious and vivacious Julia. The fact that the General was well in his nineties might have had something to do with his courtly behavior.

When he left this vale of tears, it was not because of any undue exertion. Don José de Corriero died peacefully one sunny morning in his sleep, leaving his enormous estate and title to his dearly beloved Donna Julia.

Pine-scented air wafted through the open window and the two young women breathed deeply. Ages ago the Vaudrez family had built their castle at the edge of the Montmorency forest, incorporating it and the few farms and villages that went with it into their feudal estate.

"Isn't springtime marvelous?" asked Florentine, the youngest of the two sisters, now mistress of all the Vaudrez possessions.

"Yes," answered Donna Julia with a barely stifled yawn. She was visiting her sister because family, friends, acquaintances and above all society, expected her to do so. After all, it takes a lady time to recuperate from the sudden loss of one's husband.

"You don't sound very convincing to me," said Florentine.

"Listen dear, I don't exactly know what is wrong with me, but I haven't had anything but headaches lately. I feel miserably depressed and, what worries me most, I cannot find a single earthly reason for the way I feel."

13

"Julia, dear . . ."

"No, I mean it. And you must admit, it's rather silly. After all, I am young, beautiful, rich, sought after and here I sit in a silly room, doing needlework and I am just plain bored stiff!"

"Are you grieving because of a lost love?"

"Oh, come on . . ."

"Well it is possible, you know."

"No, Florentine, as far as my emotions are concerned, I have had my share of entanglements. I gave all the love I had to give to Gaston, Count Saski—and he was not worth it. I have completely forgotten about him. Don José I loved, but in a different way. No, it is a feeling of complete emptiness and uselessness. How about you? Don't you feel the same? After all, it is two years now since you became a widow. Tell me, doesn't this fresh breeze, the smell of young pine and the sparkling sun do anything to you? Doesn't your flesh sometimes ache for companionship? You don't really believe that woman was created to just sit and pine away in loneliness? I sometimes reach the point that I don't care how rich and well respected I am. I am not asking for a big love affair, good heavens, no! But there should be some solution to this problem of physical loneliness, and I don't seem to be able to come up with one. It's driving me completely insane!"

Florentine was quiet for a while, after her older sister's unexpected outburst. Then she said, softly: "You are right, I frequently feel the same way. But don't forget that I have a young child!"

"Oh, I couldn't forget that. But you only

have to worry about him during the daytime. Your nights are free while he is asleep. Or do you sleep well, too, by any chance?"

"No, not at all, and you?"

"I have nights that I have to bite into my pillow or I would scream. Often I toss and turn and dream that I am being possessed by a wild and wonderful man. My hand will automatically go to my crotch, helping out my fantasies. The illusion makes me temporarily forget the miserable reality, though sometimes my own fantasies frighten me as much as the realities."

Florentine blushed when she heard her sister talk that way.

"There is no reason for you to blush, dear," Julia said, "because I have a very good memory."

"What do you mean by 'very good memory'?"

"I remember a certain slip of the tongue you made the day after your wedding. And good Aunt Briquart had to show you why you were still a virgin, even though you had spent your wedding night. You said, 'But dearest aunt, how could I possibly be a virgin after I have experienced such delights? Surely no one else but a man can give this to a girl?'"

"Oh, yes . . . now I remember. But how come you know about this? Where were you hidden?"

"I was in the other room, admiring your trousseau. The door was slightly ajar and through the mirror I could see what Aunt Briquart did to you as an explanation of how to enjoy the marital delights without any help of a man."

Florentine blushed deeply. Julia looked at her in a strange way, half smiling, half blushing. Then she threw her arms around her sister's neck and said softly, "Why don't we go to your boudoir, and I will show you how that indiscreet mirror was placed."

Florentine got up from her needlepoint work and the two sisters went into the room where the Colonel's wife had shown the young Madame Vaudrez the difference between fingering and fucking. And, undoubtedly because they figured that it would be senseless for the mirror to reflect what was about to happen in that boudoir, they carefully bolted the door.

"Fate must be smiling upon you," Julia said to her sister. "The memories of so many happy hours are soaked up by the walls of your home. You can spend a lifetime dreaming about them. My ecstasies have been experienced in practically every hotel on the Continent."

"Aren't they buried in your heart? Isn't that enough? Maybe you are right, I don't know. But it seems very unlikely to me that our romantic lives are already at an end. Yours has been romantic from the start, and I must admit that quite often I was very jealous of you."

"Yes, the hours of drunken passion in the arms of Gaston Saski were truly indescribable. But so was the rude awakening!"

"You must forget everything you did not like, and remember only the happiness," Madame Vaudrez told her sister, trying to get Julia out of her dark mood. "Come here, close to me, little foolish sister of mine, and I will pamper you like a baby."

And adding her deeds to the words, Florentine pulled Julia closer to her, covering her ears, eyes and lips with tender, passionate kisses. The

16

tender scene was reflected by the mirror opposite the couch.

"Look, Julia, and see how harmoniously your dark hair blends with my blonde," Florentine sighed.

"You are right," her sister said, removing combs and curlers deftly from her sister's coiffure. Florentine was equally as adept at unfurling Julia's dark tresses. The dark and the blonde hairs fell down the women's shoulders, and combined into a lovely frame for the two beautiful faces that were hugging one another.

"Ooh, look at the cute birthmark you have here on your neck," Florentine exclaimed, unbuttoning Julia's blouse, undoubtedly to get a better look at it. She kissed it tenderly. "I never knew you had one there."

"I know of one that a certain Madame Vaudrez has, but it is very cleverly hidden by two beautiful velvety globes," Julia said impishly, meanwhile feverishly trying to unhook her sister's bodice.

"Why don't we compare?" Florentine had gotten into the spirit and quickly unhooked her bodice and corset, revealing two marvelously formed breasts. Her sister exclaimed in admiration, "Oh, my! I have never seen such beauties! You are as blonde and gorgeous as I think our Mother Eve must have been. Please let me look at you in the costume she wore before she was tempted by the snake!"

"I would love to do that, but it must be mutual. In our natural costume and before the mirror. Then we can look at one another and take on any position we please."

With this and similar exclamations the two young women had begun to strip. First their

17

bodices, then their blouses fell upon the carpet, quickly followed by their corsets, underwear and stockings.

And the two beautiful female bodies in all their glory stood mother naked before the large mirror. One was the ideal blonde, the other the most perfect brunette.

"Oh, you are so beautiful!"

"You gorgeous creature, you!"

For a moment the two women looked at each other like two wrestlers who are about to start their bout. Julia put her arm around her sister's slender waist, and began to kiss the girl's neck with tender kisses, her lips touching Florentine's soft skin, fluttering like the wings of a butterfly. Florentine shivered with delight and the rosy tips of her breasts began to swell.

"Ooh, look how cute!" Julia exclaimed. "Just wait, you two, and I'll teach you some manners!" She took the tips playfully between her passionate lips and rolled them around, one after the other, in her warm mouth. Florentine sighed happily. Julia's tender kisses slowly became more firm and passionate, her hands cupping one breast and then the other, squeezing firmly while her pearly teeth nibbled the engorged tips. The younger sister was squirming wildly under her strange lover's caresses. Julia picked her up and carried her to the couch.

"I will make you a bet," Julia said, "that no one has ever done to you what I am about to do."

"And what's that?"

"Just look in the mirror, dear sister, and you'll see!"

Florentine looked and she saw her sister,

18

kneeling on the floor, while she spread Florentine's thighs with nimble fingers. Her face disappeared into the golden curls of Florentine's crotch, expertly searching for the little tickler.

"Ooh . . . what are you doing?"

"Nothing special . . . not yet . . . but before I am through you will have died with passion." Julia licked her sister's rosy, twitching clitoris and then her eager tongue disappeared deeper into the love grotto. Florentine no longer uttered mere sighs of deep satisfaction but began to stammer loose, voluptuous words.

"Ooh . . . my dear God . . . what is that . . . deeper . . . I couldn't . . . any longer . . . please, quicker . . . ooh! . . . I never knew . . . what delight . . . it's marvelous . . . quick, quick . . . deeper . . . more . . . harder, please, now . . . Ooh, God . . . My darling . . . darling, please, don't stop . . . oooh!"

"You just wait, my little dove . . . you haven't felt anything yet," Julia said, licking her lips. Then she put her head back, burying it deeply into Florentine's golden fleece, her fingers parting the moistened curls. Florentine's clitoris grew more and more rigid, as Julia's head bobbed quicker and quicker, her tongue penetrating as deeply as it could. Julia's hands strayed over her sister's belly, slowly squeezed her thighs and disappeared under her buttocks. When she felt that Florentine was about to come, she firmly squeezed one finger deeply between the crack of Florentine's buttocks, penetrating the little hole. At the same time she managed to get the clitoris into her mouth, sucking it wildly. Florentine screamed out loudly, spasmed wildly and flooded copiously.

With a deep sigh, Madame Vaudrez' head

fell back onto the pillow and she did not even answer when her sister embraced her with passionate kisses, saying, "Well now, look . . . don't fall asleep, my dear little egotist!"

But no matter how hard she needled her sister, Florentine did not react and remained limply on the couch. Julia was torn between two different feelings. She was worried about her sister's odd behavior, and she also wanted a release from her own pent-up feelings. She began to shudder and wanted to get up. But she could not. Two strong hands had taken a hold of her hips and she felt a caressing tongue trying to worm into her crotch.

"Oh, my God . . . who's that!"

"Please, dear lady, don't move," answered a familiar voice. "It's only me . . . Dorothy, your maid . . . ooh, I cannot tell you how badly I have always wanted to do this . . . only I never dared . . ."

"It seems to me that you have finally made up your mind . . . and since you have gotten off to such a good start, it would be a terrible shame to have to tell you to stop," said Julia, bending over her sister's charming breasts, at the same time giving Dorothy an opportunity to admire her firm, well developed buttocks.

Dorothy, no longer afraid of her mistress, began to try and excite Julia with the mastery of her agile tongue. It did not take long for her to succeed.

Her tongue seemed to be all over. Now here, now there, once soft and tickling, another time strong and firm. She played the crotch and crack of her mistress as if they were musical instruments. And it must be said that

20

Dorothy was a virtuoso. And her fingers, too, did not remain idle.

Such a beginning was bound to have an effect. And indeed, Julia began to squirm and groan. Florentine was staring at this strange scene which developed before her eyes. Suddenly Dorothy played her big trump. She lifted her skirts and produced a marvelous male member of fantastic proportions.

It seemed that she was very well acquainted with its use, because suddenly she introduced it into Julia's dripping fleece. The whole thing disappeared while Julia let out a scream of pleasure and surprise. Dorothy really knew how to imitate the natural movement of a powerful prick with her giant dildo.

"Oooh . . . aaah!" Julia exclaimed, seconding every movement. "It's killing me . . . I'm dying of happiness . . . what heavenly delight . . . who is flooding me with this warm jism? He's killing me, but I love every moment of it . . . aaah . . . eeeek!"

Dorothy saw that her work had reached its completion and dropped her skirts. Then she caught her mistress just in time and bedded her down, next to Florentine, on the couch.

One could have heard a pin drop in that room. The three women used this moment of silence to regain their composure. Then they looked at one another . . .

CHAPTER TWO

"I hope that my lady will forgive me, if I have done the wrong thing." Dorothy broke the shocked silence respectfully. But her behavior made it all too plain that she did not expect any punishment for what she had just done.

Dorothy was Julia's devoted chambermaid and constant companion. It seems that ages ago she was the favorite prostitute of Count Gaston Saski who had hired her to serve Julia when he took the latter as his mistress. When Count Saski went to Poland, and his aunt caught him screwing her protégée, the Count had been forced to marry the young lady. When Julia married Don José de Corriero soon thereafter, she had kept Dorothy, who was the best housekeeper anyone could wish. Julia was always full of praise for her dear companion.

But this was something new! Dorothy had always been very discreet. As any good chambermaid she was fully aware of her lady's private life. Obviously, she would never tell anyone about it, especially since Julia paid her handsomely.

"Now, Dorothy, would you please explain how you managed to get in here," Julia asked. "In the first place, I thought that you were on your way to Paris, and in the second place, I am sure that I bolted the door of Madame Vaudrez' bedroom."

"My business was taken care of sooner than I expected, and when I found the door bolted, and I heard the ladies having a good time, so to speak, I took the liberty of using the little secret door through the backstairs."

"Oh, you little hypocrite!"

Dorothy smiled.

"It happens to the best of us. It was pure coincidence that my affairs in Paris were settled so quickly, and I had honestly no intention of sneaking in the room. But I went, as I said, through the back door and, as Madame knows, in my profession I have to be able to be silent. And what I saw was so charming and attractive that I could not find the courage to leave discreetly. I watched the marvelous relationship between you and your sister but I also knew, from experience, that you, dear Madame were going to be left high and dry. Madame Vaudrez had spent so copiously and had come so often that I was afraid that she could not repay you for your services with similar passion. And therefore I decided that I would do it to you in her place."

"My dear, I am very grateful for that," said Julia, "but how could you do to me what you did? I am positive that I felt something penetrate inside me and it was definitely nothing female. I just don't understand it."

"It would be a pleasure if I could show the ladies the means I use to achieve my goals."

"Oh, please . . . yes, do," the two ladies exclaimed vivaciously.

Dorothy did not have to be told twice. She lifted her skirts high, up to her big breasts, and showed a gorgeous and firm belly. Around it was a corset which was held firmly in place with two straps around her huge white thighs. But most amazing was the contraption fixed to the corset. It was made out of resilient rubber and resembled a huge male member in a state of gorgeous erection.

"Ooh, how funny!" the ladies exclaimed.

"Wait a moment," Julia said, "I distinctly felt a warm fluid squirting into me. That could not possibly have been produced by this lifeless instrument."

"If Madame permits," Dorothy continued, "may I point out these two containers. They resemble the balls of a man, and can be filled with warm milk. When I felt that you were approaching a climax, I simply squeezed them, and squirted the warm milk into your belly. That way it produces a complete climax just as if it were a sex act between a man and a woman."

"We forgive you for the intrusion, Dorothy," Julia said.

"Madame is too good, and I swear that you can count upon my complete discretion. But if the ladies permit me to say something . . . I cannot understand for the life of me that when a woman is young, beautiful, rich and free, she wastes her time with artificial means. Actually I think that it is bad for one's health. And why should two ladies like you use such a last resort? Especially since it is so easy to get the real thing."

"Please, Dorothy, you seem to forget completely that remarriage is a very serious business."

"Marriage? Who said anything about marriage? My God, I would not dream of suggesting such a thing. No, no! No chains. Take a lover. Take a man to whom you can give yourself with body and soul as long as he pleases you and as long as he is charming!"

"But what would people say of such a steady stream of changing partners? They will excuse a more or less steady affair which looks like a marriage. I must admit that Count Saski was right; in proper society nobody is so indiscreet as to ask for a marriage certificate."

"But what if you meet someone, and you believe you are in love with him, he gives you physical satisfaction, and it is pleasant to be near him. What if he turns out to be an unappetizing lout the next morning, or—even worse, what if he cannot physically live up to the promises he implies? Then you have to let him go, you are compromised in the eyes of your acquaintances, and all this because a lover did not live up to his expectations! These unpleasant situations can easily be avoided."

"Dearest Dorothy, if you have found a remedy, please let me know about it. Because I must admit that I prefer the passionate embraces of a male above all the contrivances and fantasies we can think of."

"And I," interrupted Florentine, who was still enjoying her climax, "have never found such tremendous ecstasy, not even in the arms of my beloved Cherub!"

"What?" Julia asked, surprised. "In the arms of Cherub?"

"Yes, yes," Florentine answered, mad at herself for the slip of the tongue she had just made.

"But he is only three years old!"

"Obviously I am not talking about the child, but about his father . . . the probable one!"

"About his father! Poor old George . . . you call *him* Cherub?" Julia burst out in uncontrollable laughter. Dorothy spoke up.

"Believe me, ladies, take my word for it. A lover is much better than repeating what we have done this afternoon. I know that it destroys your health when you do it often enough."

"Nonsense! What on earth could be the difference?"

"It has a tremendous effect upon the nervous system. And I know what I am talking about, because I have successfully completed my training as midwife and nurse. As a matter of fact, I was one of the best students in the school."

"I don't want to pry into your private affairs, Dorothy, but I happen to know that my former lover, the Count Saski, considered you one of the best and most accomplished inmates of the house of Madam Lucy. And we both know that if it weren't for the affection I feel for you, you wouldn't even be a chambermaid. Then, tell me—how come you are a chambermaid today?"

"Because I was stupid and young, and through a scandal in which I unwittingly played the main role, I was expelled from school."

"Please, tell us about it, Dorothy."

"It's a pleasure, if the ladies are interested. It is now so long ago that it does not any longer hurt me, and the story really is not long.

"I had a lover to whom I was very much devoted. He, too, was a student at the school. I also had another one. I was not in love with him, though I liked him very much. And, he could do me a lot of good, because he was one of the teachers at the institution.

"One night I went with Marcel, my lover— the student—to Bullier, who had one of the most famous dance halls in Paris, 'The Hall of Lilacs.' I danced with various people and had a marvelous time. Marcel, however, did not do anything but drink, and he became very obnoxious. I wanted to go home to avoid a scandal, but he refused to accompany me. Frankly, he was barely able to stand up straight. So, I decided to leave him alone with his bottle, and go home alone. Unfortunately, I completely forgot that he had the second key to my apartment.

"I had barely walked fifty feet on the boulevard when I met Paul, my teacher."

" 'Where are you going?'

" 'Home.'

" 'That's very stupid of a young girl to go dancing alone,' he scolded, 'I'll walk you to your apartment.' Obviously, he wanted to come in, and we began to kiss and neck. He put me on the bed, undressed me, spread my thighs and tried to enter me.

"The dancing had excited me, and I allowed him to push his wonderful penis into my cunt. The joy was ecstatic and the release of my pent up emotions was so great that I grasped his huge prick and helped him plunge it into my cunt.

" 'Darling, darling,' I panted. 'Fuck me, fuck me until I bust. I am dying to have a terrible big fuck. I must feel your whole big thing in me. See if you can get your balls in, too.'

"He fucked me till my head whirled, till I almost swooned, and when I finally came, it was as if the whole universe had fallen upon me. He, too, came with a series of tremendous spurts, and finally we fell asleep.

"Early in the morning I heard a light noise Someone was trying to open the front door. Then I heard footsteps in the living room. It was Marcel, who had come over to apologize.

"I did not dare to move, and since he could not wake me out of my pretended slumber, he undressed, slipped into the bed, and fell soundly asleep. After all, he had enough wine in him to guarantee that he would not wake up soon. Paul, who was exhausted by our love bout, also slept very soundly.

"The only one who could not sleep was I. To sleep between these two men was anything but pleasant. I did not know what to do. Both would be furious upon awakening. I was sure to lose Marcel's love, and I was equally as sure that my grades for the upcoming examinations would suffer, because Paul would not be too pleased, either. In short, I panicked. I got up out of the bed quietly, packed my belongings in two suitcases, dressed quickly, and left the apartment.

"Early that morning, Marcel, who thought that I was sleeping next to him, wanted to make up and grabbed for my hidden charms. Paul, who at first thought that I wanted to be nice to him again, allowed the intimacy and reciprocated. You can imagine that he swore up a storm when he discovered a huge penis instead of my sweet little cunny. Both men got into a fight and—I heard this later from one of my neighbors—accused one another of being fairies, sodomites and queers.

"It did not become a matter for the police, however, because when the men cooled down a little, they could surmise what had happened. The whole affair became known throughout the Latin Quarter, professor and student became the laughingstock at school, and the end result was that I was expelled from school.

"Madam Lucy, who ran a house of prostitution, offered me a job. The girls in her establishment were not the run-of-the-mill whores, and she thought that I would make a valuable contribution to her house. That is how I came to know Count Saski. I still see Madam Lucy from time to time; she runs a very exclusive salon, and it is only upon recommendation that she allows her guests to enter.

"And that, my dear ladies, is the reason why I am now in your service instead of having my own consultation room, horses and carriages, my own home and a considerable income like so many of my former schoolmates."

"Well, Dorothy, if I were you I would not lose courage. After all, there is still a possibility for you to make a lot of money, because I can promise you that Florentine and I will show our gratitude if you succeed in arranging our plans for the Rue Charles V. Am I right, Florentine?"

"Absolutely! I would love to try this experiment together with you. But, dear little sister, under one condition only. That both of us from time to time . . . like today, I mean . . . is that all right with you?"

Julia kissed her sister tenderly.

Dorothy helped her mistress and Madame Vaudrez with their toilet and nobody would have guessed an hour later, when the two ladies received guests in their salon, that they had so completely given themselves to voluptuous pleasures.

Besides, Dorothy had promised them a completely new experience. She was going to try and get them an invitation to one of Madam Lucy's intimate soirees.

CHAPTER THREE

Not long after Dorothy had surprised her mistress and Madame Vaudrez in the latter's bedroom where she had screwed her mistress with a dildo, Madam Lucy gave one of her famous, intimate soirees. Julia and Florentine were lucky enough to be invited; they both went under assumed names: Pomegranate Flower and Miss Evergreen. Although it was against the rules of Madam Lucy's establishment, Dorothy had explained to her former employer that both ladies had plans for the future where these names might become very important. They only would visit Madam Lucy's establishment once, because in matters of sex both ladies were very inexperienced. Madam Lucy was flattered, and allowed the house rules to be broken, just this once.

Her small, select parties to which only a lucky few—mainly the very rich, the very important and the titled—are admitted, enjoyed among the highest circles a remarkable, or rather extremely curious, reputation. The secrecy which surrounded these gatherings had made them notorious throughout Paris, and everyone who was anyone desperately tried to get an invitation.

Dorothy, of course, belonged to the small group of friends of this hospitable lady, and she had really kept her word to wrangle an invitation out of Madam Lucy. She did not hide the fact from her mistress and Madame Vaudrez that getting the invitation had been exceedingly difficult. She also had some misgivings.

"My dearest ladies," the devoted maid said, "you may have to count on the possibility that as newcomers you may become highly involved, and I am almost afraid . . . what I mean is, once you are in Madam Lucy's salon, anything goes, and it is impossible to refuse anything. Won't you reconsider while there is still time?"

"Ah, rubbish, my dear Dorothy," Julia said. "I am not such a prude when I happen to be in the proper company, and neither is my sister. And besides, now you have really aroused our curiosity!"

Julia was not just curious but truly eager for an introduction to the home of Madam Lucy. When she was still the mistress of Count Saski she had picked up enough allusions to this famous establishment, and under no circumstances did she want to pass up the chance to see for herself what was going on. She knew full well that the happenings in Madam Lucy's house were incredibly licentious, and ladies from the finest families in Paris fought for the honor to be admitted to the odd entertainment of the intimate little groups that gathered there.

Two very important rules had to be followed strictly, exactly as laid down by the Madam of the house. In the first place, utter discretion was a must, and in the second place, everyone —without exception—had to accept the rules of whatever games were played at the particular party. If one could agree to these two stipulations, an evening of incredible delights was held out as a proper reward.

And Dorothy had told the sisters what Julia already had guessed, that whatever happened at the home of Madam Lucy was not exactly commonplace.

Madam Lucy was a widow of about forty years old, although she looked no more than thirty. She had a sister, Laura, who lived with her, and who appeared to be a few years younger. Laura was about to divorce her husband and, as far as the sisters could gather, this man lived in the colonies and made only very infrequent, short visits to Paris. Rumor had it that he lived with a Negress in Africa. Anyhow, he was very rich, and his charming wife had a considerable income.

When the two sisters, together with Dorothy, entered the salon of the beautiful Madam Lucy, they met a small gathering of about ten persons.

There was the old Count de Paliseul, a very interesting gentleman "in between the two ages," with graying temples and a tendency to become corpulent; an Officer of the General Staff, Baron Maxim de Berny, tall, blond and muscular and—as one could expect—the spoiled lover of all the courtesans and respectable women in Paris. Then there was Dorothy, well dressed and very ladylike, blonde and stately, with an enormous bosom and wide hips. Miss Elinor D. MacPherson was from the United States. She was a redhead, a real Irish devil with sea-green eyes, a wicked mouth with an incredible amount of lipstick and very beautiful pointed breasts. It was impossible to overlook this detail, if detail is the correct word. These huge things were truly remarkable, especially since the gown of this lady had the lowest plunging neckline Paris had ever seen. There was a banker, Monsieur de Lyncent, and a very pale, fragile-looking woman from Andalusia. She was Senora Padilla, who was at the party with her husband, a small, lean gentleman with pitch-black hair that seemed to be pasted down on his skull. He was the Consul from Spain. Finally there were John and Molly Teeler, brother and sister, young, very young, so much so that the sisters were beginning to doubt whether the soiree would take the course they had expected.

But then they were told that the latter two were performers; he an accomplished musician and she a so-called "plastic dancer"—one of those girls who sprinkle themselves with bronze powder and then portray all the females inhabiting Mount Olympus. They were then satisfied that the evening would fulfill their expectations.

Besides, a small speech of the gracious hostess enlightened everyone completely, and there was no doubt left in anyone's mind as to what was about to take place during the course of the coming evening.

"Ladies and gentlemen," Madam Lucy said in a low tone of voice—shortly before her little speech all the lights in the house had been doused, except for a few hidden ones which spread a discreet glow—"you want, as far as I understand from your own words or those of your friends who were kind enough to introduce you to me, to taste with me the delights which are so frequently denied to us. You and I have now gathered in this small group. All have the same thoughts about this particular subject, and it is therefore that we shall be able to enjoy our desires without undesirable results and, above all, without restraint. I have seen to it that my servants, as usual, have the night off. There will be absolutely no unwanted witnesses to the proceedings. I fervently hope they will soon start, and I beg you to use your unbridled imaginations, and to throw off all your inhibitions. After all, we have gathered here with a delightful idea in mind and I beg you not to forget this, no matter in what situation you might find yourself."

A softly murmured "Bravo" interrupted the smiling Madam Lucy.

"Now, please allow me to repeat the few most important rules of our little get together. There are actually only three. Number one: Shame is a plebian attitude. Number two: Everyone is for everyone. Number three: The ratio is three to one which means that the ladies are allowed to reach a certain delight three times. I presume that I do not have to go into detail. The gentleman can enjoy the same ecstasy only once. For further proceedings the ratio may become six to two, and so on . . . let your imaginations work, give them free rein. It is a ratio at which I arrived after many delicious experiences, and I hope that the gentlemen can be trusted upon their word of honor."

The last reminder, obviously, was only meant for the men present. It seemed that the official part of the little soiree was over, and Dorothy whispered a few little explanations, telling Julia and Florentine that everyone was expected to follow the instructions of the hostess, and that moreover the rules of the game were of the greatest benefit to the ladies.

They were gathered in a rather large living room. There was no lack of a place to sit— or rather, to lie down. The rug in the middle of the room was free of any furniture, though grouped around it were four large, oversized couches. There were several sofas in the corners of the room, and many love seats and overstuffed easy chairs. Several small tables throughout the room were loaded with bottles and plates, filled with all sorts of delicious snacks. Various exits led into smaller rooms which were discreetly lit and tastefully decorated.

The guests walked around, inspecting the various rooms, getting acquainted with one another, and slowly pairing off in small groups. If it had not been for the words of the hostess, no one would ever have thought they were amidst a rather special gathering of people.

But then came the voice of Madam Lucy again. "Gentlemen, would you care to dance? Mister Teeler, please start the music."

And the next moment, soft music filled the room and soon several couples danced to the exotic music. Maxim de Berny walked over to Florentine and invited her to dance with him. She accepted, and his strong arms embraced her passionately. He was a very good dancer.

Julia was asked by Senator Junoy. After a few dances they remained standing together and then sank down upon one of the couches.

"Did you get a little bit warm, my dears?" Again it was the voice of Lucy, clear but husky. "I believe the gentlemen should be allowed to take off their coats. And I also think that the ladies. should be permitted to unbutton their partner's flies . . ."

The two sisters were speechless. That is what one might call speeding up the proceedings! Hastily, the gentlemen, led by the Senator, that wicked creature, took off their coats.

"Well, Monsieur de Berny? And what about your tunic. That uniform must be extremely uncomfortable. And please, Madame," Lucy said to Florentine, "you will have to struggle with that hermetically sealed uniform fly!"

Florentine noticed that her partner's face reddened. "How funny," she thought, "and this is only the beginning!" But at the same time she looked around for Julia. There was her sister, sitting on the next couch, together with the little Spaniard. Madam Lucy was standing next to them, obviously repeating her invitation. It seemed that the couple needed some urging, but finally her sister stretched her hand toward the pants of Senor Padilla.

Florentine had already put her hands between the legs of her escort, and what she found there exceeded her greatest expectations.

One great sigh seemed to drift through the room. All the couples were now standing, or sitting, in a big circle. The gentlemen's behavior was still correct, though all of them were now dressed in their shirt sleeves. The ladies had their right hands extended and encircling the hardening members of their partners of that moment.

But Madam Lucy was watching carefully, and she was in full control of the entire affair.

"Well, my darlings," she said pleasantly but firmly, "I believe that the first introductions are over and done with, and I assume that you don't need my instructions any longer. I am very sure that all the gentlemen are now more than ready to pay slight compliments to their ladies. Please, gentlemen, don't hesitate. We women would love to get thoroughly acquainted with that which interests us most. Come to think of it, I would assume it to be very entertaining if the gentlemen would now take a firm hold of whatever is of greatest interest to them. Now, please, let's do it all at the same time. Grab firmly whatever charm it was that attracted you first to your female partner."

What followed was positively hilarious.

Madam Lucy's suggestions were followed to the letter. Though the women had obeyed Madam Lucy's instructions rather hesitantly and shyly, the gentlemen were more direct and firm.

Florentine looked over at Julia and Senor Padilla. And, indeed, the little Spaniard had already taken a firm hold of those charms of her sister which had undoubtedly intrigued him most, namely her perfect, delicious breasts. His brown, strong hands fingered around in Julia's low-cut gown, and he quickly succeeded in freeing one of Julia's full, well-formed breasts.

Somewhat further were the banker, de Lyncent, and the wife of the Spanish consul. Florentine could not exactly see where he had his hands, but it was easy to see that he was kissing the languishing Andalusian upon the mouth, trying to wriggle his tongue between her teeth.

"Our friend de Lyncent is a saint," a gentleman remarked. He looked like one of Ruben's fauns, with his little, twinkling eyes, his reddish face, and his full white beard. "A chaste little kiss satisfies him completely."

This remark surely did not describe the gentleman's own desires, because he had just taken a firm hold of the charms of the silver-blonde Molly Teeler who looked, with her light blonde tousled hair and big light blue eyes, like an appetizing little doll. One hand was energetically kept busy with her well-formed, obviously firm and hard bosom, and the other hand had crawled under the pretty young girl's dress. The gentleman did not even take the trouble, once he had reached his goal, to rearrange his partner's skirt, so that her marble-white upper thighs were completely uncovered. He had put his faun-like head slightly down, and was nuzzling under her armpits. It seemed to tickle her, and she burst out in a loud giggle.

"Ooh, I can't stand that . . . please . . . please . . . Oh, sir, you're tickling me too much . . . no, please, no . . . aaaah."

The slightly tortured-sounding giggle had stopped, because Count de Paliseul had let go of his partner's armpit and had begun to nibble upon her strawberry nipples which were smiling at him from her half-opened gown.

Without a doubt, one of the gentlemen, Monsieur de Laigle, knew his manners, because he was entertaining both ladies of the house. Each one was sitting on one side of him. Laura, who had opened his fly, was softly playing with his stiffening scepter, and he was tenderly stroking her full behind. At the same time his legs encircled the thighs of Madam Lucy, and it was obvious that his hand had already reached that spot which is covered with a tuft of hair.

The talented young Johnny Teeler—he could not have been more than nineteen or twenty years old—did not interrupt his soft musical playing. Nevertheless his hands no longer played waltzes, but they magically performed known and unknown singing melodies which increased the enchanted mood that now permeated the room.

And when Julia looked carefully at the dimly lit corner where he was playing, she noticed that he executed his paraphrases and melodies with only one hand. True, it was done with such virtuosity that nobody seemed to notice this. The only one who knew for sure was the American Miss Elinor because his left hand had taken a firm hold of one of her incredibly pointed breasts. She had taken it out of her dress and offered it to the piano player, holding it in both hands which made this pointed pear appear even larger. It was enchanting to behold this fascinating woman. Her well-filled yet slim figure rested upon a pair of firm, long-stemmed, gorgeous legs for which the American women are so justly famous. She had an unusual piquant face which was framed by fire red—one could almost call it indecent red —hair which contrasted strangely with her nymph-green, incredibly large eyes. It was not surprising at all that the young musician, whose fly was open like those of all the other gentlemen, showed an enormous hard-on.

Maxim de Berny, too, had taken the charming cue of the hostess without any hesitation. He had become an entirely different person ever since Florentine had liberated his enormous manhood out of its uncomfortable position. Florentine loved to caress this gigantic, swollen, stiff prick. She was dreaming about how it would fit into a certain pink-colored sheath.

His military reserve had made way for a zealous kindness. And, when the gentlemen had been asked to take possession of the charms that attracted them to their ladies, he had become more than just zealous and kind. He immediately grabbed a very firm hold of Florentine's legs.

"My dear and precious lady," his hot breath whispered into her ears, "I . . . I . . . have only seen you tonight for the first time. Oh, I am sure that you did not even notice me . . . there were so many other interesting people present . . . but ever since I saw you tonight, I have been haunted by a wild desire . . . I have dreamed passionate dreams . . . and I hope fervently that they will come true. My thoughts have been possessed by only one desire . . . to touch your legs . . . those beautiful, gorgeous, long legs. They seem to be sculptured out of marble . . ."

His strong hands firmly underscored his words, confirming that he meant what he said. But he seemed not only interested in Florentine's legs, since his hands were also very busy with her thighs and the tuft of hair in between. He paid homage to her fleece that left no doubt as to his intentions. However, it did not disturb Florentine in the least. After all, that was what she was here for, and she fully intended to make up for her years of widowhood and her years with a rather impotent husband. She felt terribly passionate and could not have cared less if the blond giant had taken immediate possession of her. In fact, she would have welcomed it. But he was still playing with her legs, her thighs, her breasts and her slowly moistening hole. When enjoyed in the proper manner, erotic delights can be continued endlessly. The passion, after all, is always there. It is only a matter of the right place and plenty of time and a willing partner. Of course, Florentine knew that a brutal, quick embrace can have its own particular charm. One can even do it standing on a front porch, while the husband is occupied with opening the door, or in a men's room of a station when one's lover is about to depart for a prolonged time, and hastily requires a last parting favor. It can even be done, she knew, in a public park, where one is protected by the impenetrable branches of the bushes.

The large room in which the thirteen people were gathered was now filled with the most unusual sounds. One could hear a peculiar soft smacking, the rustling of the silken gowns of the ladies and the starched shirts of the gentlemen. There were the loving grunts and groans of the men, and the giggling and soft moans of the women. Breathless moaning, and the panting and the gasping which left no doubt as to what was going on. Added to this was the typical, very exciting creaking of the furniture caused by the movements of the bodies that occupied them.

But the soft, enchanting music of John Teeler had stopped. In its place an occasional note was heard whenever Miss Elinor's elbows hit a key of the piano against which she was leaning while she straddled with widespread legs the lap of the young, blond piano player. In this strange position she went with him through all the motions that people usually perform when they are firmly pinned down on a mattress.

And they were not the only couple busily engaged in this particular delight. The skinny Spaniard had succeeded in inducing Dorothy to stretch out on the couch, and he was kneeling between her powerful legs. He was working a little bit too fast for Dorothy's taste, pushing his lance with such enervating speed against the girl's belly that she finally took his prick in her hands, forcing him to slow down. Her full breasts served as supports for the nervous Spaniard's outstretched arms and his skinny brown fingers voluptuously kneaded these enormous snow-white balls.

Monsieur de Laigle had put Lucy's sister in front of him. She offered her full, white buttocks up to his throbbing spear and he took possession of her behind with a certain nonchalance. Even while he penetrated her from behind, dog fashion, he refused to take his cigar out of his mouth. It was a curious sight. He fucked her, puffing his cigar, giving her enormous jolts. Laura kept very still, but breathed passionately and deeply every time the huge shaft of her partner disappeared up to the hilt into her wide open cleft.

The hostess had not yet actively joined one of the many couples. She wandered from one little group to another, now cheering them on with a witty remark, then removing a piece of clothing which might be in the way, occasionally fondling a buttock, a breast or a pair of balls, whenever such a part was uncovered.

"Well, Monsieur de Berny, I am sure that Miss Evergreen is ready for you. Don't you want to honor the lady with your, as I can observe, more than ready sword?"

At that particular moment the couple did not need these doubtlessly well-meant encouragements, because without any further ado the strong, muscular officer had pushed Florentine down upon the couch and . . .

The girl did not think that she had ever experienced such powerful thrusts ever before in her life. The blond officer had mounted her as if he were a wild stallion, and he worked her over with tremendous force while he raised her legs high. He raved madly against Florentine's belly, his balls slamming hard against her buttocks. In a very short time she felt pains as she had never before endured. But strangely enough, the pain became pleasant, and her hips started wildly gyrating, her cleft wide open, as if she was about to swallow the whole man.

His breathing was rattling, but strangely enough, though it seemed that he could hardly get enough air, he kept exclaiming exciting words. Their monotony was, at first, strange and frightening, but ultimately Florentine became as hot and passionate as she had never been.

"Aaaaah . . . finally, finally . . . now can I fuck between those legs . . . between those legs . . . I am fucking between those beautiful legs . . . between the legs of a most beautiful woman . . . aaah . . . and what have you got between those sweet, beautiful legs? A cunt . . . a cunt . . . aaaah . . . how I have longed for that little hairy honey pot of yours . . . right between your legs . . . oooh! Your legs, your legs . . . and I am fucking you right between those gorgeous legs! Ooooh . . . aaaah . . . let me die fucking between those legs . . . the legs of an angel . . . I will never take my prick out of this cunt again . . . I want to stay between your legs . . . my hard prick in your hairy cunt . . . aaah . . . how delicious to fuck that cunt between your legs . . ."

It was by now quite obvious to Florentine that her partner was particularly fascinated by her legs. It was also possible that their perfect line and form exceeded his wildest secret dreams. Anyhow, the muscular lover became wilder and wilder.

"Sweet . . . oh, how sweet . . . the way you raise those legs and spread your thighs . . . those legs . . . so that I can fuck between them . . . can you feel my balls slam against your ass? Oooh, I am fucking between the most divine legs . . . legs that seem to be praying for a harder and wilder fuck . . . I will give it to you, my love . . . I fuck that cunt . . . between your marvelous legs . . . and now you are spreading them so wide that I can put my prick in all the way . . . ooh, don't you like it, this big dong between your divine legs . . . oooh, feel how it rubs . . . oooh, my prick is at home at last . . . I am fucking you between your legs . . . I never want to stop . . . I want to fuck between your legs forever and ever . . . oooh, divine one, I am fucking you . . . between your legs . . . oooh, please, allow me to die between your legs . . ."

Florentine had to admit that it was a rather novel experience to have her legs honored in such a peculiar way, while she, as a person, did not seem particularly attracted to the officer. But, she told herself, she did not come to find eternal love; sex was enough. And as far as that was concerned, their coupling was extremely satisfactory, and they rammed their bellies voluptuously together.

The behavior of her partner reminded Florentine of a famous composer, a friend of her late husband, who had enticed his mistress—a

44

divinely talented singer—to submit to him while she was singing a well-known, very difficult aria. And ever since that day he was unable to listen to her singing without being overpowered by the wild desire to possess her while the beautiful tones ran from her lips. To make this technically possible, the couple had agreed that he would rest on his back and have his mistress with the golden throat settle down upon him so that she would be able to sing her beautiful aria while he was pushing wildly under her, listening to her enchanting voice. Occasionally he would reach a certain height which would cause in her a sour note. But, on the whole, the arrangement worked perfectly for both people.

Julia, too, was literally drowning in passion. She had come twice already, though she had masterfully succeeded in hiding this. She wanted to enjoy the precisely measured, powerful jolts of Senor Padilla to the utmost. He worked without letting up, and his powerfully swollen muscle of love penetrated deeper and deeper into her longing body with every ramrod jolt.

Dorothy kept her partner working on her incessantly while she was crying out, "Oh God, I am coming . . . I am . . . coming . . . oh, my God . . . how I . . . am coming . . . again . . . again . . . oh, God . . . I am . . . coming . . . you screw so marvelously . . . I . . . am . . . coming . . . again . . . ooh, it's fantastic . . . I am so . . . horny . . . you fuck like . . . a bull . . . aaah . . . I am . . . coming all over . . . again . . . aaaah . . . aaaah!"

It was really very enjoyable to watch all these happy people. The big, blonde woman had turned slightly sideways. One of her ex-

tremely strong and powerful long legs, covered
with a blue silk stocking, was held high up in
the air by her partner, who held on to it as if
it were a main mast of a sailboat, tossing in
the wild seas. His lower body pushed rapidly
with speedy thrusts against the widely opened
cleft of his partner. He almost squatted between her full thighs, straddling the one under him with his skinny legs as if he were riding a wild pony.

Dorothy was resting upon her mighty hips,
showing a full view of her large and imposing
behind. The gigantic cheeks shimmered milk
white in the subdued light of the room. They
jerked and palpitated continuously, pushing vi-
olently backwards against the belly of her partner, who kept pushing against her with short,
very rapid little strokes. His peter must have
sealed off her twat almost hermetically, and
Julia decided to try out this obviously very satisfying position as soon as she had the opportunity.

The wife of the thus busily engaged Spaniard was about to enjoy special delights herself.
She had been selected by the hot-blooded Count
de Paliseul. It appeared that he was more attracted to her than to the silver-blonde Molly,
and maybe he had reached his goal quicker
than expected. He was now about to experience new delights.

He was zealously bearing down upon the
tender, completely disappearing wife of the fiery
Senor Padilla. The speed of the good gentleman was surely much slower than she was used
to, but the force of his thrusts must have been
incredibly more powerful than those of the
skinny Spaniard. The Senora was whimpering

quietly, but it could have been because of incredible delight which was forcing this soft meowing out of her throat.

"Aaaaah, Monsieur, aaaah, so good you are doing it to me . . ." she almost sobbed. "It is soooo good . . . aaaah . . . aaaah . . . more, more . . . please . . . please . . . aaaah . . . ooooh . . . you satisfy me much . . . you are so much better than my husband . . . ooooh, how delicious . . . no, please, don't stop . . . it feels so good . . . more, more . . . aaaah . . ."

Her partner was as red as a boiled lobster. It was obvious that he was driving his shaft into her with his last remaining force, but it was equally as obvious that this task was not an unpleasant one for him. In fact, he was enjoying himself tremendously. This pale Andalusian woman, with her exotic beauty, had beautiful, graceful, finely chiseled legs and incredibly gorgeous, slender thighs. The panting, gasping fawn had put both legs across his shoulders and his heavy, fleshy hands gripped her small but muscular buttocks firmly, pressing them with a slow but regular rhythm against his own belly. This small woman was incredibly voluptuous, because every muscle in her small body shook and vibrated. She pushed herself against the huge man on top of her with such fervor and passion that it seemed as if her frail body consisted of one heavily tensed muscle.

The blonde beauty, the sister of the pianist, was now possessed by the horny banker. But it was not the normal position in which all the other couples were engaged. Either because of weakness, or because of perversity, the banker was busily engaged in an entirely different way. His gray haired head disappeared almost completely between the widely opened white thighs of Molly, who languidly stretched out on one of the sofas.

One could almost say that the young girl was an extraordinary beauty. Most interesting was the radiance of her appearance. Everything on her contributed to making her look like an angel. Her hair had the color of finely spun gold. The skin of her body and face was almost translucent. It was impossible to make out whether the snow of her bosom or the lilies of her thighs were whiter.

The form-fitting black silken gown, which did not hide anything on her perfect figure, was pushed up high above her waist by the horny old goat who was about to shove his facial duster into her small mother-of-pearl boudoir. It gave everyone present a peculiar feeling of tension to watch the balding gray head of the banker mix with the shimmering pubic hairs of this beautiful, innocent young girl. The zealous money lender had also pushed the gown of his willing beauty down her shoulders, thus exposing both of her full, pointed, yet very innocent looking breasts. He took this opportunity to grab them both with lustful hands, playing around with them as if they were rubber balls. From time to time he rubbed both divinely red strawberries between thumb and forefinger— the same way a lieutenant of the guards twirls his moustache—eliciting excited groans from his beautiful partner.

The beautifully formed legs of this gorgeous creature rested upon the shoulders of the old man who was kneeling before her. It was incredibly obscene and shameless. Her legs were held up high and bent backwards. The high heels of her black lacquered, piquant shoes pierced deeply into the back of the totally absorbed man, slowly pushing him closer toward her. There was actually no need for her to do so, because the head of the insatiable banker had almost completely disappeared into her widely opened cleft, and he looked for all the world like an animal trainer, sticking his head into the widely opened, hungry jaws of a lion.

* * *

Truly, the night afforded so much variety, and it was so exciting, that the sisters could not, with the best will in the world, recall every single detail. They also had no recollection how, after a certain time, the four enormous couches that formed a circle around the rug in the middle of the room were suddenly transformed into a gigantic resting place. Upon this enormous area, the couples sought and found one another. The watchful hostess saw to it that her guests' activities did not degenerate into selfish single acts, which would have robbed the people present of their sense of belonging, and which would have prevented the mutual orgy which now followed.

The bodies of the participants at this sensational soiree soon formed an incredibly complete whole. They all formed one huge body with an enormous amount of arms, thighs, legs; a great, living thing—breathing, panting, moaning, groaning and sighing out of its many lungs. It offered breasts in all shapes—huge one, pendulous ones, pear-shaped and melon-shaped, dark-skinned and milk white globes, with an equal variety of nipples—from tiny strawberry-red ones to big, jutting firm ones,

49

inviting to be sucked and bitten. Buttocks, cunts, mouths, pricks, and balls in delightful opulence invited the many groping hands and eager mouths. The people who had become this huge thing moving on the enormous bed seemed to consist entirely of semen-filled cunts and mouths, throbbing pricks and slamming bellies. Now rule number two achieved its full, wonderful result. "Everyone for everyone" took on its true meaning.

It would have been impossible not to follow this rule, once caught up in this indescribably wonderful mass of naked and almost naked bodies. It was impossible for any of the participants to avoid the embrace of the nearest neighbor, or to escape from a throbbing prick, a yawning cunt, or the voluptuously grabbing hands of someone.

But then, nobody had the slightest intention of doing such a thing. They did everything in their power to pull as much flesh as they possibly could, to hold as many hands as was bearable and to kiss eagerly the many hungry mouths and tongues. The smell of sweat and semen worked like a powerful aphrodisiac. The groans and cries of the others seemed to spur flagging powers to even greater deeds. The two sisters found themselves now on top and then under many bodies. Sometimes they were pressed against one another and, then again, against another partner. They were in one continual hot embrace, completely entangled. It was a mystery how the various couples, or rather groups, always succeeded in getting loose from each other only to form new connections, new couplings with new partners, trying new and different techniques. They did things, and

50

enjoyed them, which they had hitherto never thought possible.

The most incredible combinations were formed by all these steaming hot bodies! The permeating smells of come, perfume, body odors from armpits, cunts and pricks were unbearably exciting.

Everything was mixed, from the most primitive wild grabs to the most refined techniques. And each deed caused ripples of delight, running the complete gamut from voluptuous desire to gasping climax . . . over and over again. The hot spark would fly from body to body, jumping through the entire group, using the nerves of these people as if they were one single medium.

Whenever on one end of the enormous bed a female body jerked in the spasms of an incredible climax, shuddering as if tortured with unbearable pains, the next moment a body on the other side would groan and jerk, coming equally as ecstatically, as if an electric jolt had passed through the entire mass of bodies in the short span of a single second.

Florentine was no longer pinned down and fucked by the massive, muscular body of Maxim de Berny, and Julia had long since lost Senor Padilla who had had his delights both with her and Dorothy. It seemed that all the male participants of this peculiar soiree at one time or another had deposited their seed in the more than willing laps of Florentine and Julia. The two sisters, who had, so far, lived a chaste life, were reluctant to ever get off their backs.

In the wild group which the guests of Madam Lucy now formed, it was next to impossible to recognize even the most intimate partner of the moment, though the girls tried to identify some of them. But how should they know whose mighty member was pushing and jolting from the back against their sopping cunts? They were thrown across the heaving belly of another, like helpless booty slung across the back of a wild stallion, while at the same time they were trying to swallow someone's throbbing manhood that was trying to impale their widely opened mouths. Julia thought that it must have been young Teeler who was stretched out next to the officer, but her hands were caught, left and right, between their wildly banging bodies, so she could hardly be sure.

And who was working her over with such vehemence? Judging by the technique, and the words he muttered, it must have been Maxim de Berny, who had spent the earlier part of that evening ripping her sister Florentine apart. On the other hand, she suspected that it could be Dorothy who had strapped on her dildo.

There . . . oooh . . . just now . . . Julia had just started to climax and already the jolting prick had squirted into her and was about to pull out of her hotly desiring quim. She was just beginning to feel sorry for herself when suddenly two powerful arms pulled her thighs even wider apart and another throbbing prick penetrated her hospitably moistened grotto . . . how delicious! Her new lover, with renewed vigor, continued the task of replacement, jolting and jarring her wildly shivering insides. She was drowning, floating in voluptuous delights she had never known before. Her wild desire temporarily quieted down with the regular thrusts. Suddenly she felt a pair of hot lips take possession of her tickler, and the head below her formed an exciting buffer for another partner who was giving it to her from behind.

Florentine, on the other side of the bed, stretched out one hand which was just released by one of her partners. There! Wasn't that the heavy club of our insatiable faun? Yes, indeed! And before she fully realized what was happening, it had already pushed itself halfway between her lips. Then, suddenly, Florentine began to bob her head wildly, trying to swallow it all, wanting to have this gorgeous throbbing member deep in her throat. She sucked some precious drops from it and then someone else pushed her greedy mouth aside.

The heavy cylinder, which for a short moment lay there like an orphan upon his belly, disappeared into a wide, very moist opening, barely needing the help of someone's guiding hand. And now, in the place of the soft mouth of Florentine, another, even softer pair of lips encircled the throbbing flesh pole of the elderly gentleman, speeding up and down without stopping.

Florentine was incredibly fascinated to be allowed to witness this variation of coupling, and she tried to give both the heavy prick as well as the encircling lips as much pleasure as she could.

It is impossible to describe the heady atmosphere that ruled the orgy room. The air seemed to boil satanically. Continuous, almost frightening gasps, shrill screams, and tortured sighs filled the air. The silence which now and then fell was even more sinister. And then, suddenly, a thumping rhythm would set in whenever several couples started to hump and fuck each other again. Accompanied by the creaking of the furniture, one could hear fanatical hands slap naked flesh, the rubbing of nude bodies slamming together, and the slurping of voluptuous lips. Now and then could be heard the characteristic sound of a softening penis slipping out of a vagina, or someone's hardened nipples slipping out of puckering lips.

Most characteristic, and also most exciting, were the spontaneous exclamations. Sometimes they were involuntary, while others were said with the specific purpose of giving vent to the wild urge of having everybody take part in the enjoyment of a particular act. Even the rather reticent wife of the Spaniard called out her feelings without shame. While she was busily engaged upon this jolting and shuddering altar of lust and passion, she chanced to come upon her husband. He was just about to attack Laura, the sister of the hostess who herself was engaged in a battle to take on the enormous prick of the blond officer.

The Senora called out in wild ecstasy, "Miguel . . . he screws me delightfully . . . I tell you, his prick is as heavy as the spear of Saint Isidore . . . aaah . . . aaah, darling Miguel, I love it sooo much . . . aaaaah . . . aaaah . . . you, Miguel . . . Miguel . . . I have to . . . please, quick . . . quick! Tell me, darling, are you getting fucked as heavenly as I? Quick . . . quick . . . it . . . is . . . so . . ." Since she started to come at that moment the rest of her confessions stuck in her gurgling throat.

Some of them were less lyrical with their expressions. The redheaded Elinor was positively obscene. Her true character showed itself when she tried to spur her partner, or rather partners, to ever greater efforts.

"Why don't you fuck me harder . . . come on, let me feel that you have a goddamn hard-on in my cunt! I said harder, you dirty son-of-a-bitch! Come on, I want to be screwed . . . put it in deeper, harder . . . ball me as if your worthless life depends on it . . . stick it in deeper . . . is it in? Jesus, I can't even feel your balls slam against my ass . . . faster . . . deeper and quicker. Come on, who can give me a real good fuck? I want to be raped as if you were a bunch of horny cossacks who haven't seen a cunt in years! I don't want you to shove it in like a gentleman . . . ram it up my cunt like a cowboy . . ."

She veritably screamed, foaming at the mouth, "I am horny, so goddamned horny! Isn't there a prick among this damned bunch that knows how to fuck well? Come here with it . . . I'll stick it into my cunt myself . . . quick . . . quicker! Can't you hurry it, come on, fuck me . . . my cunt is burning up . . . Give me that hot dong . . . screw me to pieces . . . shove it up my cunt harder . . . deeper!"

And the raving redhead snatched furiously at the dripping prick of the Spaniard who had just pulled it out of Laura.

"Haaaah . . . here's one that just came . . . boy, did that one come! That's how I want to be screwed . . . come on, you bastards . . . I'm horny, and I want to get fucked . . . by all of you! One prick after the other . . . stick in your dong . . . dammit . . . yeah, that's it . . . one after the other . . . I want to be laid by every goddamned prick in the house . . . deep . . . hard . . . and quick! Hurry, hurry . . .

that's it . . . work it in deeper . . . a little bit faster . . . deeper . . . aaaaah, that feels good. Finally I'm beginning to feel good . . . this one fucks me even better . . . come on . . . I . . . want . . . to . . . harder, dammit, deeper . . . a little more . . . aaaah . . . aaaah . . . ooooh! Eeeeek!"

Her voice suddenly gave out, but not because this terribly horny creature had reached a climax, or even found some satisfaction. One of the gentlemen had suddenly put his swollen penis into her opened mouth, penetrating deeply into her throat. This cork effectively stopped this wellspring of Anglo-Saxon lechery.

* * *

There was one more special climax to this evening worth mentioning. It was not that the mood of excitement had abated, but the participants were becoming slightly tired. Yet, it was obvious that all had a desire for stronger excitement. In short, the following proposition was eagerly applauded by all, even before it had been completely uttered. Young Johnny Teeler was going to fuck his own sister! Strangely enough, this had not yet happened, and it must have been by pure chance. It could never have been because brother and sister avoided each other on purpose. This would have been simply impossible in the ingenious mixing machine upon which everybody had been romping around. But now they had to make up for their omission.

"Oh, Johnny," Molly suddenly blushed, "should we really do . . . this?"

Like all the others, Julia and Florentine were very curious to see how the young and handsome Englishman would react to the proposition.

"Children, you simply have to do it. It really makes no difference. Everyone here has fucked everyone else. Even the married couples have seen their partners screwed by others. And that does not happen too often, either!" This argument was brought forth by Miss MacPherson, who had finally caught her breath. She was still busy gagging the juices of her last partner, which dribbled out of the corners of her mouth.

"Molly, don't forget our cardinal rule, 'Everyone for everyone!' After all, we can't help that you two happen to be brother and sister. After all, Laura and I are sisters. That never prevented us from showing affection for one another. And, as I understand, the ladies Pomegranate Flower and Miss Evergreen, who are sisters, have a nice thing going together, too! Think of all the famous lovers in history and mythology who were brother and sister. Why, even the Pharaohs of Egypt and the Incas in Peru couldn't get married *unless* they were brother and sister. Now, come on . . . don't be so ridiculously bashful! And don't tell me that the two of you have never slept in one bed together when you were kids. Even without touching each other!"

"Yes . . . that is true. We also used to play around a little . . . I mean, with our . . . with our . . . But what you order us to do, we have never done," Molly stuttered excitedly.

"Well then," Madam Lucy resumed, "you two will just have to catch up and rectify that mistake. Oh, come on, Johnny, don't be a party pooper. Here is Molly . . . she is gorgeous . . . who cares that she is your sister. Throw her on her back and get it over with!"

The resolute Madam Lucy, with Laura's help, had already pressed the blonde girl down upon the huge bed, holding her nude body firmly upon the pillows.

"Here, Laura, help me. Take a hold of her legs and pull them a little apart. No, not roughly, just hold her lightly. It will only take a few seconds of good banging and she will lap it up."

"Oh, please, dear Madam Lucy! Don't you know that it is a deadly sin? We have never done a thing like that! Johnny . . . don't . . . no . . . don't! You are my own brother! No . . . don't . . . no, no, no . . . how can you dare to force me . . . no . . . don't . . . no . . . no . . . ooooh . . . I . . . aaah . . . Johnny . . . no . . . oooh, Johnny, Johnny!"

During her last exclamation, her brother pierced his heavily swollen prick deeply into her belly. It was a beautiful performance, even though the fear of the precious little girl was touching. Her brother, one could easily see, had no difficulties whatsoever. It could have been possible that he had been waiting for a long time for an opportunity like this one. He possibly had lusted after his own sister for years, eagerly wanting to enjoy her charms. Anyhow, his zeal and his powerful thrusts were proof enough that as far as he was concerned, passion was more powerful than prudish conventions.

The guests formed a circle around the balling couple. Everybody was curious and wanted to see everything. It was no longer necessary to hold the girl down. She was panting wildly with every thrust and her thighs opened wider and wider. The two formed a nice, charming couple. It gave everyone great satisfaction to know that Molly, who was getting the hang of it, would from now on allow her brother to screw her more often.

"Ooh, Johnny, how good . . . how good . . . how beautiful it feels to do it with you . . . Please, please, go deeper my sweet, sweet Johnny! Do you remember . . . how we . . . used to . . . play . . . husband and wife? But this is really much better . . . it is . . . really good . . . only . . . this . . . way . . . please, Johnny . . . go on, deeper . . . push deeper . . . only . . . a few more . . . I have to . . . come! Aaaah . . . aaaaah! Oh, Johnny . . . lover . . . I am . . . coming . . . oooh, Johnny . . . don't stop now . . . go deeper, quicker . . . please, please . . . Johnny, screw me some more . . . fuck me, dear . . . darling brother . . . I want to come again . . . fuck . . . fuck me . . . aaah . . . you . . . have . . . to . . . fuck me . . . often . . . and hard! Always, always . . . I want you . . . to fuck me . . . always . . . tell me, Johnny dear . . . promise that you will . . . always screw me like this . . . aaaah . . . aaaaah . . . you . . . you . . . you!"

And the charming little sister of Johnny Teeler had reached her climax.

CHAPTER FOUR

A few months later, a small group of gentlemen were sitting in the small salon of one of those exclusive Parisian clubs. They were some famous gentlemen of Paris society, namely de Lyncent, de Melreuse, de Laigle, de Resdorff and the Officer of the General Staff, Maxim de Berny.

All these men of the world were sitting, or standing, around the Count de Paliseul, who sat in a leather easy chair telling one of his famous tales. Most men listened to him, smiling, because they knew his habit of exaggeration.

"Oh, this Raoul," murmured Melreuse, "the most fantastic adventures always seem to happen to him! I envy his powerful imagination."

"Oh, you don't believe me, gentlemen? Well, I swear upon my word of honor that everything happened exactly the way I am telling it to you," answered the young man.

"Come on, Raoul, things like that happened in the time of mail coaches and highway robberies, exciting abductions of young ladies, and all that sort of rot. But nowadays! Please, don't make us laugh. Why are you trying to pull the wool over our eyes? But, since you know how to tell a story with such brilliance and passion, we will allow you to go on with your report," laughed de Lyncent.

"Oh, no, gentlemen! If this is your attitude toward my story, and I swear it is a true story, I prefer to remain silent."

"Now, now, you don't have to get mad at us!"

"All right, gentlemen," a few voices spoke up, "since it concerns a true, true story, the first one who interrupts again must pay a fine!"

"We are all ears, friend Paliseul. Continue your story. So far, all we know is that for the past three days you have found among your mail a letter on English paper, written in a very correct style and instead of a seal or initials it was closed with a golden sphinx. We also know that the said letters smelled delicious and were perfumed with a particular smell you had never smelled before. Now, what could be more natural than when you had opened those letters, that you read that the mysterious writer ordered you—if you had the courage and the discretion—to walk at two o'clock in the afternoon on the Avenue MacMahon and to contact there a woman who would give you a calling card with that same delicious perfume and printed with a golden sphinx. That would have to convince you that the woman was sent by your mysterious writer."

"My dear Melreuse, you will never become Attorney General for France. You have just rattled off what I have already told. Maybe you can become a court stenographer."

"What do you want, my friend? I am used to the wild stories my children tell their nanny. But come on, Paliseul, I have brought everyone up to date with your story, and now it is your turn to continue with your novel."

"I'll be more than happy. I went to the secret rendezvous, and despite the fact that I was supposed to walk, I took a cab. I only wanted to see what was going on. But I won't bore you gentlemen with unimportant details."

"So far, you haven't been doing anything else but that," someone interrupted.

"The fine, the fine! Pay your fine!" called the others. "Now please, gentlemen, we have promised to be quiet, and let Raoul tell his story."

"To fulfill the condition that I had to walk I ordered my coachman to stop in the Rue Tilsit, from where I strolled into the Avenue Mac-Mahon.

"I waited for about ten minutes while I was trying to figure out with whom I was going to be brought in contact. It could be with one of those society ladies who are reaching the dangerous age, and who have to prove to themselves that they are still as attractive as ever. It could be a woman who had heard stories about my reputation in the boudoir, and it could even be a virgin who had become dissatisfied with that state of affairs, and who was now trying to contact me through a matchmaker.

"I began, frankly, to lose interest. My thoughts were turning somber and morbid, because who wants to go through all the humdrum just for a simple lay. After all, the lady in question seemed to be desperate. Lord knows that I have more affairs than my poor manhood can handle.

"But then, suddenly, a thought hit me like a flash of lightning, giving me a ray of hope. I decided not to return to my carriage in the Rue Tilsit, but to wait some more.

"After all, the style of the letter, the elegant paper, and the exquisite and obviously very expensive perfume did not point to one of those sordid affairs we all know so well.

"I had just reached that happy conclusion

when my daydreams were disturbed by the arrival of an elegant coach, obviously made in England. The elegant vehicle, pulled by two splendid horses, was driven by a Negro coachman. It drove very quickly, and I could see that the livery of the Negro was black with gold borders and the buttons on his uniform were golden sphinxes.

"The coach stopped suddenly, about twenty paces from where I was standing. I must admit that my heart was pounding a little faster than normal. 'Who could possibly come out of that beautiful coach?' I asked myself."

"Now, really, my dear Paliseul. We can all fully understand how you felt at this particular moment. But can you please come down to the facts, you eternal blabbermouth. Hurry up with that story!"

"Oh, drop dead. Beautiful needlework has never yet ruined a beautiful gown!"

"He'll never finish that story, if we keep interrupting him," said de Resdorff.

"As I said," Paliseul continued, "a lady came out of the carriage. She was of uncertain age, wore a heavy veil, and she was dressed in one of those solid, well made gowns which makes it almost impossible to guess rank or standing. If that is going to be my lady love, I have been had, I thought, and I'll disappear as quickly as I can.

"This thought became even firmer when I noticed that the woman was of the same black race as the coachman.

"The Negress looked me over very carefully, quickly crossed over to where I stood and handed me the promised calling card.

" 'Monsieur de Paliseul?' she asked, though

63

it was obvious that the old witch must have known who I was.

" 'That's me, Madame.' I answered this unattractive creature coldly.

" 'Would my lord the Count please check the perfume, so that he may know that this card is legitimate.'

" 'That is not necessary. I believe you at your word, and I also hope that you finally will explain this whole mystery to me. I feel as if we are conspirators. Did you at least bring a blond wig and a black mask? That's the only things I forgot to bring with me. I must admit that in this role I am a newcomer.'

" 'These little remedies are unnecessary. The wings of love will be enough to cloak us.'

"She had said 'us', and I shuddered at the horrible thought that crossed my mind.

" 'All right,' I answered, 'if I have to fight under the wings of the Almighty, there is very little I can do about it. But, my dearest lady, I am not smart enough at guessing games, and I would be greatly obliged if you would clear up this whole mystery!'

" 'With pleasure,' she answered. 'It's the reason that I am here.'

" 'Then, please, don't let me wait any longer!'

" 'My mission is only to be the go-between.'

"Though I had counted on this, I must admit that I breathed a lot more freely to have her confirm it. At least I did not any longer mistrust her motives, though I became extremely curious and returned to my first assumption. Who would be the lady of society in need of money, in return for which she would be willing to offer me her charms?

64

" 'My mistress,' the Negro woman continued, 'is a foreigner.'

" 'Who does not come from this country?'

" 'It is as your Grace says, and I can also see that you are in a very humorous mood.'

" 'And who of the great minds of Montmartre or Belville has taught your mistress the subtlety of our beautiful French language?'

" 'Madame,' she continued, 'belongs to the high aristocracy of her country, and because of her position she cannot afford to have intimate connections in her own circles, if I may say so.'

" 'You may. Your explanations are a little bit obscure, but I think that the gist of it is perfectly clear.'

" 'Your Grace does understand what I am saying?'

" 'Completely. What is Madame's name?'

" 'Pomegranate Flower.'

" 'I'll be damned, if you will pardon the expression. That is a name as burning hot as the sun of Andalusia. And it is obvious to me that anyone with a name like that is incapable of loving loneliness, Miss . . .'

" 'Felicitas, at your service, Count de Paliseul.'

" 'Is your mistress beautiful, young and witty? You do not have to tell me whether she is a blonde or a brunette. Her pseudonym tells me that she must have the dark eyes of a woman of Madrid, and her hair is black as the feathers of a raven.'

" 'That is indeed a wonderful guess, Monsieur. And I might add that she is one of the most beautiful women in Paris. Moreover, she is only twenty-five years old.'

" 'That is the age when the fruits are juiciest, Miss Felicitas.'

" 'Unfortunately, she must be very careful in combining her personal desires with the conventions of society.'

" 'You must admit, Miss Felicitas, that this desirable creature is taking a tremendous risk. Can you imagine what would happen if I were not a man of honor?'

" 'As far as that is concerned, my lord . . . my mistress knows you very well.'

" 'Well, now, that's the limit! This beautiful stranger knows me?'

" 'Absolutely!'

" 'Pooh!'

" 'Oh yes, she has known you for almost two years.'

"I must have looked very incredulous, but Miss Felicitas told me so many intimate things from my private life that I could no longer doubt that the unknown beauty from that far country knew me through and through.

" 'In that case,' I answered, 'I can only be very grateful to Madame Pomegranate Flower that her beautiful eyes have fallen upon me, and that she has considered me worthy of being her companion.'

" 'Yes, but there is one more thing.'

" 'And that is?'

" 'That you must give your word as a nobleman never to try and find out who she is.'

" 'Discretion is my noble virture. I accept that condition, and I add to it that, if I ever were to meet Madame Pomegranate Flower socially, I would never give away that I know her, unless she greets me first.'

" 'That is still not enough. You must also

66

promise never to try to remove the domino mask which she always wears.'

" 'Now, that is the most ridiculous thing I have ever heard of! Your mistress, I am sorry to say, must have lost her mind during her travels. She greatly desires, if I am to believe you, an intimate friend and even then she intends to wear a veil or a mask?'

" 'Yes, but only as far as her face is concerned.'

" 'Aah . . . only her face?'

" 'Yes!'

" 'And what about the rest?'

" 'That might be, if the circumstances are proper, be unveiled.'

" 'Good. I hope that this will make up for not being able to see her lovely face.' "

"That Paliseul is the worst bandit I ever heard," groaned de Melreuse.

"I agree. Completely without shame. It's positively indecent," added de Laigle.

"A fine for both of you," exclaimed de Lyncent. "You two have promised to shut up! Come on, Paliseul, don't let us wait. Your story is getting very interesting."

" 'Do you mean to tell me,' " de Paliseul continued, " 'that Madame Pomegranate Flower would show herself to me without any clothes on?'

" 'Did Eve when she talked to the snake in the Garden of Eden wear any costume?'

" 'No, she definitely did not. What you say makes a lot of sense and I promise happily to do whatever you have asked me. But I must admit that I am burning with desire to see this divine goddess, who, if she is as incredibly beautiful as you say, dares to show herself in her natural state.'

" 'In that case all I have to do is invite Your Grace in the name of my mistress for a light supper. I will be here promptly at nine o'clock tonight to drive Your Grace to the home of my mistress.'

"I already had an engagement for that particular night, but the adventure was too exotic to pass up. I promised the black chambermaid that I would be there on time, at the same time thinking what exactly was going to happen.

"It did not seem that it was a matter of money, for it had not even been brought up. My beautiful paramour-to-be seemed to know me very well, and therefore, she should have known that I can be had for flowers and candy, which really aren't very valuable. Was this woman merely eccentric, or was I about to be ambushed?

"I decided that the latter possibility was not at all impossible, and I decided to carry a gun with me."

"Oh, my dear God. Sometimes his imagination goes too far! Jesus, man, we are living in the nineteenth century! Things like that just don't happen any longer. You may have some money, but you aren't worth all that trouble," murmured a voice in the background.

"At exactly nine o'clock"—de Paliseul decided to ignore the nasty remark—"I was at the same spot on the Avenue MacMahon, and a few minutes later the equipage came speeding along the empty boulevard. The golden sphinx was painted on the door, and I must admit that it seemed to me that the Negress was painted black, also.

68

"I had barely seated myself, when she drew the curtains, and it was impossible for me to see where we were driving. We must have been riding crisscross through the city for at least a half hour when I suddenly heard a whistle. I shivered.

" 'Don't be afraid,' said my companion smilingly. 'The coachman is deaf and dumb and this is the sign for the doorman to open the gate. We have arrived.'

"And indeed, I could hear the creaking of a heavy iron gate, and the coach drove through some sort of tunnel. We stopped in front of a large, marble staircase with hand forged railings. It was a very expensive estate.

"Enormous vases of porcelain were placed everywhere, filled with fresh flowers. It gave the place a festive look which was enhanced by the many lanterns which lit the entire front of the building. But, gentlemen, I am afraid that I am tiring you with my long story. Maybe I'd better stop."

"That is like interrupting a serial in a newspaper. To be continued—just at the moment that it gets spicy. Come on, Paliseul, let's hear the rest of it."

"Fine with me, but let me catch my breath first."

"Waiter, bring something to drink for our friend here! I think that he was hinting at our lack of hospitality. And we can't hear a sexy story out of a parched throat!"

CHAPTER FIVE

"The house which I was about to enter was by no means a new or modern building. It was, however, obviously a very well kept estate, and maintaining it must have cost the owner a fortune. Moreover, it was located in a quiet section of the city, because I did not hear a sound coming from the streets. The house was quiet, almost dead, which made the many flowers and the brilliant lights look eerie.

" 'Would your Grace please walk up these stairs?' Felicitas, who had preceded me, opened the door to a small waiting room which was covered with Oriental tapestries and rugs.

"The Negro woman announced the Count de Paliseul, opened yet another door, and I believed myself transported to one of those fabulous places mentioned in the stories of a Thousand and One Nights.

"On a couch, at the other end of the room, a woman was resting. And what a woman! She wore an enchanting negligee made out of white velvet and red silk. Only a dress designer drunk with love, could have dreamed up such a gown. Her face was covered with a domino mask, but her arms were naked, sticking out of the red silk. I had never seen such beautiful arms. They could have belonged to the Venus de Milo!

"Her firm, ample bosom peeked through a thin, silken blouse which was barely held together by a few ruby-colored ribbons. She wore some fresh flowers in her hair.

"Her entire dress was so incredibly voluptuous that I was struck dumb. And, my friends, you know that this hardly ever happens to me. Nevertheless, there was nothing in her demeanor, or dress, which reminded me of a courtesan. Not even of a very, very expensive one.

"I was standing in a huge, high-ceilinged room which was completely covered with a rose-colored velvet, upon which flowers and arabesques were embroidered. Tapestries, artfully folded, were hanging from the ceiling, losing themselves in the corners, making the room look even more enormous. Comfortable furniture was artfully grouped in the room, and exquisite objects of art were everywhere."

" 'A poor hermit welcomes you,' said a melodious voice, and an aristocratic little hand was offered me. She wore a wedding band.

" 'A hermit! Possible! However, it seems to me that your hermit's existence has in no way interfered with your becoming an aesthete,' I said, giving her my most seductive smile. 'But I would be extremely grateful,' I added, 'if this beautiful hermit would allow me to share the abode with her. I will do anything in my power to make it very attractive for both of us.'

" 'You may not wish that after a couple of days.'

"I looked at her carefully. She was a beautifully built woman. And her whole demeanor betrayed that she was a member of high society. I waved my hand as a protest to her insinuation.

" 'Sit down next to me,' my charming hostess said, 'and let's talk some while tea is being served.'

"I sat down, quite close to my secretive lady, and she showed neither embarrassment nor the usual shyness which always seems to be unavoidable when two members of opposite sex are suddenly thrown together.

"We were sitting intimately close together when the black Felicitas announced that a small supper had been served. Meanwhile, Madame Pomegranate Flower and I had been talking as if we had known each other for years. Our conversation was very flippant, to say the least, especially since my lady seemed to know a lot about many of the little secrets of Parisian society. Even though she was a foreigner, she was extremely up to date on all the scandals that were going on, and she seemed to be well acquainted with many of the skeletons that are hiding in important Parisian closets. Once in a while she would throw in a few foreign sounding phrases, but my knowledge of languages is not so great that I could identify them. I can therefore only assume that they were properly used.

"My beautiful Pomegranate Flower offered me her arm. She trembled slightly. She led me into a tiny dining room where a table had been set with a fine, elegant supper for two. And who can describe my incredible surprise when I could see, through a double door, an enormous bedroom with a gigantic bed, a heavy velvet canopy and a few Algerian lamps which cast a mysterious spell in the room.

"I was now sure that all my fears had been unfounded, and I decided to enjoy whatever the evening might bring. I recognized the symptoms and was full of anticipation.

" 'Dear Count,' said my beautiful lady friend, after we had finished our lobster, liver paté, and strong tea, 'let's do away with the ceremonies. What is your name?'

72

" 'For you, my beautiful Pomegranate Flower, my name is Raoul.'

" 'Well, then, my dear Raoul, what would you think about a little stay in my domain?'

" 'I think that would make me the happiest man in Paris, and the thought alone of this intoxicating possibility practically makes me lose my head.'

"And to prove my words, I kissed her beautiful breasts softly. They had somehow slipped out of her blouse, and the erecting nipples were driving me wild.

"The young woman made a slight jerking motion, but it was so unnoticeable that I knew immediately that I had gotten the green light.

"A few moments later we ate from the same plate, and drank from the same glass. Pomegranate Flower was sitting on my lap, and she gave my wandering hands complete free play. The pink ribbons of her blouse were in my way, and I pulled them loose. The blouse fell to the floor, revealing beautiful white globes which were tipped by hardening strawberry nipples.

"A simple jewel held her tiny corset. I unclasped it and then . . . my entire being still shivers at the memory . . . my arm encircled her submissive, voluptuous body. I could feel spasms of incredible passion jolt through her entire being.

" 'Pomegranate, my adorable one,' I whispered, 'I see you today for the first time, and already I am smitten by an unquenchable love.'

"The delicious woman smiled and threw her arms around my neck.

" 'Ooh, your lips are so fiery! I want to devour them!' My lips pressed against hers, my tongue crawled into her warm mouth, and the way she reciprocated drove me out of my senses, making the bulge in my pants larger than it had been in a long time.

"'And your breasts, oh lovely lady, what precious marvels . . . I have promised to respect that horrible mask you are wearing. But what about the rest?'

"'It is all yours,' a sweet, trembling voice whispered.

"'You must be the most beautiful woman in the world,' I said. 'But, alas, my friends call me a doubting Thomas. I would like to see, before I believe.'

"The negligee, too, slipped to the floor, revealing one of the most beautiful female bodies I have ever seen. Her shoulders were beautifully rounded, and as milk-white as her breasts. I was absolutely speechless. I felt her skin shiver and crawl and the breasts begin to firm, jutting provocatively forward. My wild, passionate kisses made any conversation impossible.

"Another clasp, on her thigh, held a pair of Turkish harem pants. I unclipped it, and the last vestige of her clothing slipped to the floor. The divine creature was sitting fully naked on my lap. Her skin was now flushed with desire, and her kisses became extremely passionate.

"'Pomegranate,' I whispered, pointing at the bed which seemed to be waiting for us, 'dear, beautiful and exotic flower . . . up to bed . . . for a beautiful bout of wonderful love! Shall we?'

"'Yes,' my hostess whispered almost inaudibly.

"And I carried her, without interrupting my passionate caresses, toward the enticing bed-

74

room. I carefully laid my booty down upon the huge bed, divested myself rapidly of my own clothing, and soon our legs were happily intertwined.

"I satisfied my desire to kiss her breasts and nibble her hardened strawberry nipples to the fullest, and held those beautiful arms firmly against my own.

"My mysterious lady love behaved like a love starved wife. It was as if I were her husband who had just returned from a year's travel.

" 'Kiss me, oh, please, kiss me everywhere,' she panted, writhing upon the huge bed.

"I complied more than willingly and both of us manifested our satisfaction with sighs and little cries of pleasure. I no longer wondered about the incredible strangeness of the whole situation. I was too busy enjoying the treat Madame Pomegranate offered me. I had no more thoughts about the engagement I had broken for that night, because I knew that nothing in the world could have afforded greater carnal delights than what I was tasting upon the enormous bed.

"I seized the nipples in my mouth, biting them playfully. She was trembling in my arms. She arched her breasts toward me, obviously wanting me to go on biting them. She almost spasmed at the touch of my lips, and it became clear to me that this ravishing lady had been love starved. I began to caress her, at first lightly. I ran my hands over her skin, from thighs to neck, from buttocks to back. She was now shuddering uncontrollably, fanning the fires of my own passion till I could no longer control them.

"I fondled her marvelous breasts at great length and then, almost savagely, I grabbed them, pinched them, digging my fingers deeply into their milk whiteness.

"She uttered deep little moans. Then she slid one nipple between my fingers, and I began to rub it. In an uncontrollable movement, she seized my head, pressing it against her belly. I ran my tongue over it, lingering around her navel, drawing deep moans from Pomegranate.

"I tried to engulf an entire breast in my mouth, and she asked me to suck her lower. I gladly obeyed, and I licked her nudity tirelessly. My ministrations were driving her mad, and she begged me to suck her still lower. Obviously, I could not resist such a charming request, and my caresses were making her almost go out of her mind. I had never seen such passion, and the aphrodisiac was incredible. I have always been able to retain my composure while dallying with a lady, but now it became quite impossible for me to retain my dignity.

"When she arched her back, offering me her secret love spot, my desire had become so great that I leaned forward, running my tongue around her little hole and rosy lips. We were both terribly excited.

"I licked the border of her hole, advancing a little, but just when my tongue was slipping into the opening, I withdrew and went back to her navel and belly. I could see that my little game was bringing her to the breaking point. And frankly, I was no longer able to hold myself back, though I had planned to spend the entire night making love to this incredibly beautiful, mysterious creature.

"We were both writhing with lust. I parted her beautiful white thighs, revealing a pink flower of incredible delicacy, encircled by raven-black pubic hairs. I kneeled on my knees between them.

"My manhood was incredibly stiff and had never been so large before. She leaned forward and brought the tip of my member up to her slit. She let out a cry of delight.

"By now I had lost all reason. I seized my throbbing prick and placed it in her cunny. She sighed with ecstasy, grabbed my hands as if to thank me for what I had done. I lowered myself completely. She pressed herself firmly against me, and our hot, steaming bodies began to tremble. We were covered with sweat, and my panting chest was pressed against her throbbing bosom. My fingers caressed her thighs, her glorious buttocks, and even the little hole nestled between their crack. It sent shivers up and down her spine.

"I cannot go into any more details, because I would be unable to get up from this chair, my friends. But let me tell you, that in our passion, our tongues tried to swallow one another, and our hands mutually explored every tiny crevice of our bodies.

"I introduced my member gently, slowly shoving it inward, till I had reached her up to the hilt. She moaned with joy as she felt my rod slipping into her. I began to move slowly, penetrating her as deeply as I could. But, suddenly, I was no longer in control of myself. I threw my head back, and almost screamed.

" 'At last, my dear love, my Pomegranate

. . . it's marvelous! We are fucking, it's marvelous!'

"She was moving wildly under me, without restraint. I felt an extraordinary exaltation rising within me. Then a wave of great passion submerged me, and I could feel that her entire body began to spasm, and we both tasted supreme ecstasy at the same moment. We let out a cry of great pleasure.

"It was a passion as I have never felt before. Never have I held such a young, glowing and beautiful female in my arms who had absolutely no reins on her unbridled lust.

" 'Will I ever meet you again?' I whispered.

" 'Possibly, my sweetheart, Raoul,' she murmured sleepily.

"Who is Pomegranate Flower? I am afraid that I will never find out. One thing is for sure, she is a woman, completely without any prejudices. And not only does she know how to be taken, but she also knows how to give. My friends, I left this mysterious home with my head in seventh heaven. I was totally exhausted. One thing is sure, I would be the most unhappy man on earth if I were never to see her again."

"What?" the little gathering that had been absorbed by Raoul de Paliseul's story exclaimed. "What do you mean, 'never to see her again!' Do you believe that this mysterious Pomegranate Flower wanted only one passionate night of love? Would she be capable of denying herself any subsequent ones?"

"I don't know. I honestly have no idea. When I said good-bye to her, I obviously asked when we would meet again. And she answered with a mysterious smile, 'When the sphinx writes you again.' And I am still waiting for that letter."

"Well, my dear Raoul, one or two nights of decent rest won't do you any harm. Those deep rings around your eyes are positively indecent, especially now that we know for sure how you got them. You have simply made too much love."

During the entire story, Maxim de Berny had not said a single word. From time to time the officer would look in his friend's direction with a mysterious smile on his face. When Raoul had finished his story, the officer walked over to the young Count, offered him his hand, saying,

"My compliments, Raoul, for your gift of storytelling. It is swinging, full of elegantly turned phrases, a melodious voice and an absolutely thrilling imagination. But please, my dear friend, don't try to swindle us, and that's what you were trying to do. And, what's even worse . . . you are an ostentatious, swaggering braggart."

"Well, goddammit, man . . . that is strong language, and I demand satisfaction."

"It is true, I am not exaggerating. Because I, too, know the mysterious woman. I know all about the golden sphinx, the large estate with flowers and lanterns. And, since I was there myself, I know for sure that you cannot have spent the night there!"

"That remark surpasses all bounds of good taste!"

"As you wish. But it is nevertheless true, and I can prove it."

The small circle of people held their breath.

It was a very long time ago that a similar sensation had shaken the club.

"Proof? I beg of you . . . what proof?" Raoul exclaimed, slightly nervous and worried.

"Now, now, let's not lose our heads!" De Melreuse, as usual, tried to calm everyone down. "Let's go over some of the details of the story once more. What day were you there, Raoul?"

"On the sixth."

"And you, Maxim?"

"On the sixth."

"And you both had supper and tea?"

"Of course!" the gentlemen answered simultaneously.

"All right, it's Maxim's turn."

"As far as I am concerned, the entire story Raoul has given was true up to a certain point. He was right about the exotically perfumed letter, sealed with a golden sphinx, the Negro coachman and the black chambermaid, and also about the perfumed calling card which I hereby show as proof."

"And here," Raoul said feverishly, "is mine!"

"So, gentlemen, be happy! Both of you were nominated, and both of you were selected!" It was de Melreuse again, who tried his best to avoid a bloody fight.

"It couldn't have been at the same hour . . ." someone interjected.

Maxim spoke up again. "Raoul gives very enticing details. However, there is one thing wrong with them. They are positively untrue! The name of the ravishing and mysterious lady was not Pomegranate Flower, but Evergreen. And she has never been near the scorching sun of the Iberian Peninsula, either! On the contrary, she is a divine creature of a far Northern country. She represents the most enchanting moonlit night. In other words, she is the most ravishing blonde one can possibly imagine. And after I had unraveled her out of Lord knows how many yards of finest linen, I beheld an Eve who had just descended from the snow capped tops of the mountain. A totally innocent woman, who was only curious. The surprise, expressed by her virginal innocence could not possibly have been faked by any courtesan. There was nothing fiery and passionate about her, but she was very cuddly and as innocently playful as a young kitten. As a matter of fact, she is so much woman that it was almost sacrilege to be a man next to this enchanting creature."

"God preserve us," said de Laigle and de Resdorff to one another. "These two are out of their minds with passion!"

"Yes," de Resdorff said, "and if you ask me, they are not only infatuated, they are falling deeply in love with women they don't even know."

"Maxim, listen," said de Laigle who was more or less the unofficial president of the Club de Topinambours, "this whole affair is so filled with mystery, that our club cannot stand idly by and have such a thing happen in Paris. Especially if it involves a secret where our combined honor demands that we unravel it! It is simply the duty of our club!"

"Our friend Raoul maintains upon his honor that he has wallowed in seventh heaven with a divine brunette. And you, dear Maxim, are just as positive that you have tasted the delights of heaven in the same house, at the same hour, with a delicious blonde. Gentlemen, now

81

please, be reasonable. Don't you think that you have been the victim of an extremely cunning matchmaker?"

"Impossible," both young men exclaimed simultaneously. "Nothing of the sort! Even the meanest servants refused to take money from us!"

"And I," Raoul said, slightly blushing, "received a letter in the mail with a substantial check which, oh, how stupid of me, I had discreetly put down upon one of the tables."

"Mystery on top of mystery."

"Yes," Raoul said, "and it is a mystery that excites me to the point where it is driving me insane!"

"Me, too," Maxim added, "and I promise that I will not leave a stone unturned to get to the bottom of this seemingly impenetrable mystery. Day after tomorrow I will keep eyes and ears open, that I can promise you."

"What?" de Paliseul asked jealously. "Do you have another meeting promised for the day after tomorrow?"

"Yes . . ."

"Did you receive another sphinx letter today?"

"No, but before we separated, she definitely promised me another rendezvous."

"Dammit! I should have done the same! Why didn't I think of that? You were much smarter than I."

"And what about your lady friend? Didn't she say, 'Possibly'?"

"I have been dreaming about that ever since she whispered it to me. Are you supposed to meet her again in the Avenue MacMahon?"

"No, this time I am supposed to . . . but,

wait a moment. I have promised to be discreet and secretive, and I am not going to reward the favors of the beautiful lady Evergreen with an indiscretion. She wants to maintain her incognito, and it is not up to me to lead you lecherous gentlemen to her secret abode."

These words evoked a storm of protests. "And what about the solidarity of our club? What about that, hah . . . can you tell us?"

"For once I shall forget about that solidarity. Moreover, the Good Book says, 'Seek and ye shall find.' I advise my dear friends to turn these divinely inspired words into deeds and if you can come up with anything, remember, dear friends, 'Finders keepers . . . losers weepers.' As far as I am concerned I leave whatever plan of action you decide upon entirely up to the discretion of the club. Just don't expect me to help you."

And with these words, Maxim de Berny left the Club de Topinambours.

After he had left, Raoul remained pouting in the big leather chair. Finally he said, somewhat irritated, "Now what on earth . . . this Maxim has all the luck in the world. What does he have, I ask you, that makes him such a prize among women?"

"My dear de Paliseul, I am glad that your father cannot hear this. He still prides himself on his prowess, and he is convinced that his son is firmly in his footsteps. And, after what we have heard tonight, it seems to me that you have the least reason to complain about Maxim." De Melreuse had, like all the other gentlemen, thoughts about nothing but women. They could not care less what types of women, as long as they had all the attributes of the weaker sex, and were willing to part with their favors. The stories of Raoul and Maxim had gotten everyone of the members of the Club de Topinambours very willing and eager. Unfortunately, not all were sure that they would be able to get some, and therefore, Raoul's pouting remark had put a sharp edge in the voice of de Melreuse.

"I . . . I . . . did not mean to say that . . ." de Paliseul stuttered, "and, besides, you know . . . with me those affairs never last long. I can't help it, and I don't know why it is. But once, at the most twice, and then they have lost their interest. I am discarded. And he!"

"Listen, young man, count your blessings. Many of us here are discarded before we are even selected. Believe me, a woman is an unpredictable creature. There is an old proverb that says, 'A woman's heart is never fair; only a fool puts trust in long hair.' Let it be a consolation to you, my friend. Maybe you are not capable of evoking eternal passion, but it saves you the trouble of getting rid of undesirable fetters."

"I am glad you are trying to lift my spirits. I have to leave now, gentlemen; I am waiting for word of my beloved Pomegranate Flower. But I can promise you one thing right now. I shan't be a hog about my little secret—like our friend Maxim!"

CHAPTER SIX

The Club de Topinambours was not the only place that night where confessions and confidences were exchanged.

In a little boudoir on the Boulevard St. Michel sat the two women who had caused the gentlemen so many headaches and heartbreaks. Their whispered conversation was repeatedly interrupted with a clear, happy laughter.

"Why," Florentine asked her sister, "didn't you come to Charmettes yesterday to tell me everything about your experiences of that previous night?"

"Well, I was surprised not to find you in the carriage, because I did use the secret stairs of our mysterious Buenretiro, exactly as Dorothy had told me to do."

"And I had asked Dorothy to let you know. Do you think she forgot about it?"

"Impossible, your chambermaid never forgets anything. She did tell me that you were very tired. Of course, I did not believe that at all. What was the matter?"

"My dear God, nothing of importance. I had to make a whole series of social visits. Besides, there was a lot to think about."

"Like what?"

"About the cliffhangers and the dangers that are part of these adventures. I wonder if those constantly changing scenes will really dispel the boredom of being a widow."

"Were you disappointed that night?"

"More or less. God knows I tried hard, but I must admit that I did not even begin to feel the delights in the arms of Raoul which I would feel by merely looking at Gaston. I did, of course, reach a climax. The physical sensation was pleasant while it lasted, but the moment he was off me, it had disappeared. His old father at that orgy we had was infinitely better."

"Oh, I hope that Maxim will never recognize me from Madam Lucy's place."

"No, Dorothy has assured me, that the heavy aphrodisiac effect of these goings-on produces some form of amnesia. It seems that the mind refuses to believe that things like that truly happen. Moreover, the light was such that I hardly recognized my own maid and sister."

Florentine seemed to breathe easier.

"No," Julia continued, "as far as I am concerned I must admit that I made a grave mistake. What can I say? One thing is for sure; I never want to see that big, blond, conceited lout again. He is just a perennial mixer. All interest in him is gone the moment you turn away from him. His looks just promise more than the poor creature can deliver. I don't know whether it is a lack of mutual attraction, whether it is him, or me . . . and frankly, I don't care. I don't even want to talk about him any longer. Yesterday, for instance, I was at a soiree at the home of Madame de Bourmond. I danced twice with him, we had the most asinine conversation, and all that time I looked at him, thinking, 'What if he knew?' "

"You mean that he really did not recognize you?"

"Not in the least! Our precautions are absolutely foolproof. But now you tell me, darling, how was your evening?"

"Well, frankly, I had selected him because he was so wild and so divine at Madam Lucy's. But now I am even more enchanted with him. He is an entirely different person . . ."

"Aren't they all?" murmured Julia.

"He is charming, obliging, kind and—above all—delicate. In his arms I have tasted all the happiness one can expect in love. At least, as far as a man is concerned. I am afraid about one thing only . . ."

"And that is that little Cherub will remain your only child. Am I right?"

"You must admit that it is a point which one cannot lightly overlook."

"Oh, come on! Trust your luck. If you don't dare to gamble, you will never have a chance to win! And even if it were to happen, all we have to do is to make a little trip, and the whole affair would be over and done with. In other words, you are going to see Maxim de Berny again?"

"Tomorrow! And I am so overjoyed at the thought that I can hardly wait. Because, unless I am terribly mistaken, this man knows how to make love. He makes love exactly the way it should be done."

"If it is so different from the tremendous screwing he gave you at Madam Lucy's, then what on earth in your opinion *is* the proper way of making love?"

"Well, it consists far more of certain sweet nothings than . . ."

"Oh, you poor child! What a miserable system to live on! Don't you realize that these enchanting preliminaries are only designed to whet your appetite? You don't walk away from a table hungry after you have nibbled a few snacks, do you? You can't just enjoy a few pre-liminaries of love, and then have your partner walk away from you! And not only that! For heaven's sake, dear sister, don't start convincing yourself that such is the natural and desirable state of your love life! You would wind up a nervous wreck!"

"Oh, no, no! One only has to know what to do when the appetite has been aroused."

"That sounds good. And do you know how? It's almost amusing, dear Florentine. I hope that it is not some offbeat little secret my Dorothy has told you?"

"Oh, no, not at all. On the contrary, Dorothy insists that using artificial means might kill me, or at least it would age me years before my time. But she did show me some exercises with my thighs, recommending this as one of the means which nature so generously provides to reach a healthy orgasm. But I do admit that this would not shut out the possibility that I could fall deeply in love with Maxim. If he were only capable of understanding me completely."

"Sister, dear, you want too much. I hope that you won't give away our little secret."

"Of course not."

"Please, don't forget it. It is terribly difficult to keep secrets from a lover with whom you are sharing your bed."

"And whom are you going to invite the next time?" Florentine wanted to change the subject. "After all, the poor young Count de Paliseul has fallen from your graces!"

"Oh I don't know, yet. I'll think about it."

"Fine, while you think about it, I am going

to take my little Cherub for a walk in the Jardins des Luxembourg."

The two sisters each went their own way, and Julia ordered her driver to take her to the Salon des Beaux-Arts where, just a few days before, a new art exhibition had opened.

It was quite obvious that the show had opened only very recently, because the place was crowded, not only with artists and art lovers, but above all with those people who want to be seen at the "right places" in Parisian society. That they far outnumbered the real connoisseurs was immediately obvious when one caught snatches of their meaningless chatter while they strolled past the various exhibitions.

Madame de Corriero was not an artist in the real sense of the word. She could barely hold a brush, and she had not the slightest idea of how to hold a chisel. But her sense of beauty and poetry was natural and highly developed. She was especially entranced by those works of art where the artist had obviously poured his heart out, even though his work might not be acceptable by conventional standards.

She walked, rather aimlessly, through the exhibition halls, looking left and right. How she would shrug her shoulder and then she would suddenly be captivated by something she saw, losing herself in reverie for many minutes.

Suddenly she stopped in front of a huge painting. She was afraid that the judges had ranked it at the bottom of the list, but she was captivated by the enchanting picture. It was nothing complicated—a forest scene, a big tree and a young couple in love. But it was this young, loving couple which caught her attention. The artist had succeeded in capturing this wonderful moment for two lovers when the world stops, and there is no one but themselves left in the entire universe. Though the painting had many technical mistakes, the artist had succeeded perfectly in showing a woman completely absorbed in the man she loves, and a man for whom the world consists only of his female partner. A ray of the setting sun brushed across the face of a beautiful young man in love.

Julia opened her catalogue to check who might be the painter. She fully intended to acquire this beautiful work. But suddenly she started, because before her, in the flesh and smiling, stood the young man from the painting. He greeted her with a mixture of respect and amusement.

"Since the painting seems to interest you, Madame, allow me to save you the trouble of looking up the name of the man who committed this deed. Michael Lompret, at your service, and I hope that you like me as much now as when I was considerably younger."

Michael Lompret, the young man from the painting, had indeed matured in the way the painting had promised. He was no longer in the early spring of his life, but had reached the stage of summer—in full glory. He was tall, slim, wide-shouldered, and his hands were slender yet strong. It was obvious that his arms and legs were powerful. He was the perfect picture of elegant strength. His sharp features were framed by beautiful black curls, and his little beard was reddish and carefully trimmed, leaving his strong, red lips free. Ooh, those lips! They seemed to be made for kissing.

The clear blue eyes of the young man stared in open admiration at Madame de Corriero. They lit up at what they saw, which might not have been socially acceptable, but it sent shivers up Julia's spine, and it left no doubt what the young man would do if given only the slightest encouragement. Julia tried to regain her composure.

"Sir," she said, slightly reserved, yet without pride, "I am very grateful for your assistance, but, please, don't let me take up your time simply because I was momentarily surprised by the likeness of you and the young man in the painting."

"You don't know how happy you make me, Madame. You think that I look like this boy? That makes me at least ten years younger."

"It is not a coincidence?"

"No, no, that was me at the age of twenty. And a little girl from the country, my first love. I believe she was sixteen," he added with a melancholy smile.

"You mean that you are the painter?"

"I told you that I have either the honor or the misfortune to be the one."

"I would call it fortune, Monsieur Lompret," Julia smlied. "This painting personifies the spring of your productive years, and may be the beginning of your fame. It is obvious, though, that you have not yet reached your peak. But I have become curious, and I would like to know how the story in the painting ended."

Michael hesitated a moment, and then he said, "It is impossible to set the clock back. We cannot, no matter how much we would like to, let fleeting time stop for one single second. Time has completed its banal destruction.

91

Like a beautiful rose, she lived only one summer. Every year, on the anniversary of that first kiss, I exhibit the painting I did when I heard that she was no longer alive. I did have great expectations from this work of art and did not expect the Art Commission to hide it away in this miserable little corner."

"It did not prevent me from discovering it."

"True . . . maybe I should rejoice instead of complaining."

"As a matter of fact, if I can get the artist's permission, I have every intention of buying this wonderful painting."

"Sell it? To you? Such a beautiful lady? Madame, that is against nature. I would be enormously pleased, though, if you would accept it as a gift . . ."

"That," interrupted Julia quickly, "is a matter between me and the Art Commission with whom I intend to deal. Monsieur Michael, it was a pleasure having met you, and I hope that the feeling was mutual." And with these words Julia de Corriero seemed to have ended the conversation.

"But I would never forgive myself, if I could not see you again."

"See me again? What gives you that idea?"

"I can think of no reason why that should be so strange. I admit that I am an artist, and not a man of rank. But when I meet a woman who looks like Venus herself, I simply lose my head—of course, only as far as the prejudices of society are concerned. I promise that I would never lose respect, and I have already begun to adore you. I can feel that you are taking possession of my mind and heart. As a matter of fact, I can feel it clearly."

"Really," encountered Julia with a smile. "And may I ask, if you are so much in love all of a sudden, are you in the habit of watching what you are doing?"

"But naturally! Because I am only in love when I can adore!"

"You better watch what you say, sir. You have already told me that you adore me . . ."

"How do I know what I am saying! All I can see is that you are about to walk away from me, and it tears out my heart!"

"Now, that would be too bad; I could not have such slaughter on my conscience. Well, since you have assured me that you will respect me, I could decide to . . ."

"You could decide what? Oh, please, speak!"

"I could put you in a position to teach me your theories about love. They seem to me a notch above the average, and they are clearly unconventional. I am intrigued."

"Oh, how sweet of you! Unfortunately, it is a long story, and I am afraid that the exhibition is about to close."

"You are right. What a pity. And the world is so evil-thinking. You may not be aware of the demands of society."

"Madame, I am the son of General Lompret," the young man said proudly.

"Well, in that case, there are seemingly no objections for us to meet when the exhibition closes in a few minutes. My carriage will be waiting for you at the exit."

Michael was a little bit stunned at the sudden turn of events, but he was tremendously pleased when the splendid equipage spirited him and the beautiful woman away from Paris.

"Sir," Julia said, as Paris disappeared in the

distance, "you know that I am eagerly awaiting your explanations about the theory of love. I am all ears."

"Madame, how could you, since you obviously possess a brilliant mind and spirit, talk so cold-bloodedly about the one and only true religion. The religion of the heart, based upon the adoration of beauty and the search for the highest fulfillment of love."

"You must admit that this religion has a tinge of paganism."

"Paganism must have been marvelous! All the religions that followed have only shown us how beautiful paganism was. A time when men were men, instead of groveling eunuchs. The people in those times must have been beautiful."

"You seem to be making quite a case!"

"Madame, everything that makes my heart go quicker is worth my making love to it. I am an artist. My feelings are my own, and it is my responsibility to make them as beautiful as possible. All things that are not directly related to nature are bad. There is a strange and compelling relationship between an artist's feelings, his mind and his body. It has to be in harmony, or he is miserable and cannot create the beautiful things he dreams of. True, I admit that quite often it is a physical desire and a physical satisfaction which brings us our best inspiration. But, alas, society does not always allow us to give full rein to our imagination."

His vibrant voice, his passionate looks and the implications of his speech charged the interior of the small carriage with a large amount of electricity which was now waiting to be discharged.

"You know that the best way to convince me," Madame de Corriero smiled, "is to prove to me that you truly belong to that small, select group who know how to love."

"I have always tried to follow the admonition in the Gospels, 'Do unto others as you would have them do unto you.' "

"With the best will of the world, I couldn't possibly want more. Tell me something, have you ever found anyone who was a complete soundboard to your feelings? You must have searched long enough."

"Unfortunately, never. Whenever I thought to behold the perfect woman, she disappeared like a mirage. I am afraid that I shall die without ever having tasted the perfection of love about which I dream."

"Oh? I would not give up all hope, if I were you."

"I hope you don't find me too forward, when I admit that I had hoped to find my ideal when I saw you this afternoon at the exhibition. You are not an ordinary woman, and you, too, know that one must be slightly mad in order to be completely in love. Two souls cannot mingle unless the bodies have become one."

Julia was visibly moved by Michael's forceful speech, and she did not pull away her hand when he put his strong fingers around hers. He took her in his arms and kissed her tenderly at first, then more passionately, and finally his hot lips pressed vibrantly against her trembling mouth, his tongue searching for the moist cavity, brushing against her pearly-white teeth. She let him do with her as he pleased, floating as if in a dream. All she could think about was to tenderly nibble on his earlobe and play with the tip of her tongue around his cheeks, neck and massive shoulders.

Suddenly the carriage stopped. Julia scribbled a few lines on a card, put the card in an envelope and handed it to a servant who was waiting outside the carriage.

"Give this to her Ladyship, immediately." Then she changed her mind. "Wait, help us out of the coach, and drive up to the house."

Carriage and servant disappeared in the distance and Michael was alone with Madame de Corriero at the edge of a forest.

"If I am not too impudent," he said, "where are we?"

"On the other side of Bondy Forest," the young woman answered with a smile. "Are you afraid?"

"Only for what I might do . . . but, don't be afraid, I won't do it."

"I would not be afraid. On the contrary! You are giving me an entirely new perspective, and you have shown me that love can exist in a form which I had hitherto never thought possible."

"You are much too charming never to have been loved, and too sensitive never to have given it."

"I am not denying that. But nothing has ever made my heart go quicker than the vision you have given me. It makes me feel a little sad, because I am afraid that only those who can conceive of these lofty ideals will be able to enjoy the greatest happiness."

"And would you allow me . . ."

"What?"

"To introduce you to this supreme ecstasy?"

"And would you think wrongly of me when I ask you to come with me?"

"To where?"

"My home, of course. Any other place would be unthinkable."

"I could not think of anything more pleasant. But, please, dear lady friend, we have known each other, it seems to me, for ages now, and I still do not know your name. I cannot keep calling you Madame.'"

"Call me Madcap."

"Madcap? That's no name for you! You are a lady of high society, that is obvious! But, if you want, Madcap it is!"

"That's just fine, friend Michael. Now, give me your strong arm, and let's walk into that direction!"

"Company! March," Michael exclaimed happily. The adventure began to intrigue him more and more.

Soon they entered one of those long driveways, bordered by giant elm trees, which led to a Louis XIII castle, modernized, with fountains, waterfowl, exotic trees . . . needless to repeat ourselves, dear reader, it is obvious that the couple had arrived at Charmettes.

"What a beautiful mansion," Michael exclaimed. "How happy you must be to live here!"

"This is not my home," Julia quickly answered, "it belongs to a friend of mine who is on a vacation, and who has asked me to stay here a while."

"Before I enter," Michael said, "you must promise me to visit me in my atelier."

"I would love that."

The carriage which had brought Julia and her newfound lover had now taken Florentine to the home on the Boulevard St. Michel. The servants had strict orders to treat Julia as if she were the Lady of the Manor.

Dinner was ready to be served, and both Julia and Michael were hungry from the long trip. They talked about poetry, art, some of the artists were praised to heaven, and others were cast in the depth of hell.

Dinner was over and Julia arose. Michael, too, got up, and Julia said to him, "Why don't you lie down on the couch and make yourself comfortable?"

Curious, he did as he was told. He stretched out on his back, pillowing his head on his arm, watching her feline movements. She slowly removed her dress, carelessly dropping it on the floor. Next came her bodice, her chemise, and finally she was draped only in a thin, gauze garment. Michael caught his breath at the provocative sensuality that radiated from his Madcap. He could clearly discern the sumptuous, proud, jutting globes of her breasts, the dark coral aureoles and, in their sweet centers, crinkly, ripely developed nipples. The filmy, thin garment clung to her hips, buttocks and upper thighs like a second skin. She turned slightly to one side and his eyes glistened at the sight of those two tightly set, upstanding and rounded, resilient bottom cheeks. She slowly removed her shoes and stockings. Her buttocks quivered and contracted in a way that showed the ambery, shadowy succulence of their separation. For the moment, she stood with her back to him, then her hands reached back to the bandeau which fastened the garment. It fluttered to the floor and she turned slowly to face him. Her breasts surged out, rising and falling very quickly. The satiny skin was flawless, velvety smooth, and her naked nipples were larger than he had first supposed them, partially hardened because of her erotic excitement.

The curving goblet of her belly was kissed deeply and widely by the umbilical niche, and then came the thick, curly raven-black triangle of fleece which covered the appetizingly plump, soft pink lips of her delicious Venus mound. She moved slowly toward him, asking demurely, "Do I please you, Michael?"

"All you have to do is use your eyes for an answer, my darling Madcap," he answered hoarsely. Julia's eyes glinted, because his cock was thrusting out with ferocious obstinacy. The turgid, dark-blue veins surged against the taut skin of his shaft.

"My goodness, I guess I do at that," she murmured. She knelt down before him and her lips grazed the huge pink-skinned knob. He felt her bestow a series of rapid little kisses all over it, and his enormous weapon tilted up higher so that she had to lift her head to follow it. He cupped her flushed, warm cheeks with his hands, watching her intently. A tremendous excitement flowed through his body when he watched this beautiful woman perform her oral admiration on his prick.

He whispered, "Enough, my darling . . . I . . . I . . . can't hold it much longer."

She smiled. "Can we do it this way?"

"You mean with you on top? Recommended for lazy lovers. Dear Madcap, I am completely in your powers. You are the mistress of ceremonies in your own home. Go ahead . . . you lead, and I will follow."

Julia knelt on the couch, moving slowly between his accommodating, widened thighs. She reached down her left hand to his tool, taking hold of the middle of the pulsating shaft. With thumb and forefinger of her other hand she slowly parted the soft, fleshy lips of her slit. Then, very slowly, tantalizingly, she lowered herself upon Michael's throbbing, impaling prick. He closed his eyes, shuddering with delight as he felt the tight, hot clamp of her love shaft cover his wildly throbbing organ. He hoped fervently that he would be able to hold himself in, because he did not want to spoil this wonderful experience by coming right now.

"Aaah . . . little Madcap . . . that is wonderful. Oh, you gorgeous little miracle . . . now that you have it all inside you, come down here where I can hold onto you. I want to show you that we are fully matched."

Michael was housed to the hilt inside Julia's tight, hot quim. Their pubic hairs merged in an exquisitely exciting friction. Slowly Julia sank down over Michael's broad chest, her ripe, juicy breasts mashing against his swelling muscles, locking her velvety smooth arms under his powerful shoulders, fusing her avid, warm and moist mouth to his. His hands gripped her full buttocks, squeezing her tightly. Experimentally, slowly, Julia arched herself a little and Michael felt his cock retreat from its delicious, warm haven. Then, with a little gasp of ecstasy, she returned all of him to her bower.

Michael took a deep breath, and then he began to join his rhythm to that of his newfound mistress. The naked beauty on top of him began to wriggle, undulate and squirm. She arched herself, only to sink back down on him

100

with ever-quickening movements. His rigid ramrod burrowed savagely into the convulsing channel behind her moistening quim.

Michael began to pant. He could feel the wild spasms of his little Madcap. His fingers dug deeper into the satiny bottom globes, regulating her movements now, guessing from the weavings and contractions of her voluptuous bare backside the precise tempo of her self-impalement.

"Give . . . my darling Madcap . . . give," he almost shouted. "Don't worry about my keeping up with you. I am ready anytime . . . yes . . . now, now! Aaah!!!"

He felt the torrential, explosive power in his loins break past his power of self-control while, at the same moment, Julia, her eyes rolling, humid and glazed, uttered hoarse and wordless cries of incredible rapture. She ground herself against him, her nails dug hard in his back as his fingers kneaded her buttocks. The quake seized them both and nearly threw them to the floor. Entwined, mouth crushing against mouth and tongues slithering together, they lay motionless together for an eternity. Only the faint sound of tiny, sobbing breaths escaped them.

Finally they got up. Julia threw a huge, Persian scarf around her shoulders, which covered her completely. Michael began to put on his clothes.

"Who you are, my dearest Madcap, I do not know. I do know that I have just felt within my grasp the heavenly moments I have always waited for. You do not have to tell me, ever, if you don't want to, what your name is. What could a name tell me that I do not know about you already. But please, my dear Madcap, assure me again that I have your solid promise. Will you visit me at my studio? Shall we have breakfast together? And can I say that I hope to see you soon?"

"My dear friend, I always keep my word. I shall see you the day after tomorrow."

Michael left, his heart filled with song and joy. Julia went to the suite she always occupied when she visited Charmettes. She, too, discovered that her heart was no longer empty. She could barely count the hours till she would be together again with her divine artist.

CHAPTER SEVEN

While Julia was exploring the ways of love with Michael Lompret, her sister was busily engaged with Maxim de Berny. She had taken up much of her time, ably assisted by Dorothy, to furnish the place in such a way as to give enough hints to Maxim how she expected to be loved. The tremendous screwing he had given her at Madam Lucy's party was still vivid in her memory. She had loved every moment of it, once his enormous tool had found its way into her belly, but the fear of getting with child prevented her from wanting it that way again.

Thus, Maxim had to be taught. He had never recognized her, and therefore Florentine had completely reorganized her little boudoir.

When Dorothy let the young man enter, the room indicated with statuettes and pictures what many people do not dare to say openly. It said that love was not merely a raw and quick way of male satisfaction. It said that there was more to lovemaking than to just screw away on top of each other and then roll away sleepily and satisfied. It implied that there was another way of giving a certain Lady Evergreen the greatest pleasure and ecstasy in a manner which some people call sinful and sick.

But Florentine had told herself with the utmost logic that the entire affair was not for the satisfaction of a certain Maxim de Berny, but for the greatest pleasure of the widow Vaudrez. What she did in that house in Paris was strictly for her own satisfaction.

"Why," she had asked herself, "should I endure all sorts of caresses and lovemaking I don't like, and hardly ever receive what I crave? In that case," she continued her justifying monologue of so many sleepless nights, "I might as well get married again, and then I won't have to be afraid of any embarrassing mishaps. If Maxim does not want to follow my wishes, the sphinx will have to remain a sphinx to him, and I shall have to look out for another lover. I wonder what Julia is up to. She asked me so suddenly and without any warning to leave Charmettes. Oh, well, I'm glad that the new reception room here is completed, and tomorrow we can exchange our experiences again."

It was almost as important to Florentine to relive her experiences by telling them to Julia to the last detail, as it was to have the experience. Sometimes Julia worried about her beautiful blonde sister, hoping fervently that the virile Maxim de Berny would succeed in breaking down Florentine's basic coldness. If she had known what Dorothy's advice would be, she would surely have given her trusted maid a severe tongue lashing.

As it was, Dorothy guided Maxim into the little reception room where the two women intended to have him cool his heels for a while. It was a small room, the walls covered with soft green silk. Strings of gilded flowers connected the eight corners. A long, oriental couch covered with the same green silk was built along the walls. A crystal and porcelain chandelier hanging from the center of the ceiling threw its clear light on the statuary grouped around the room, and the pictures hanging from the wall. A small heater in the middle of the room wafted an aromatic smell.

"Madame offers her excuses for being tardy," Dorothy said, "and begs his Lordship to wait for her." She left Maxim alone. Soon, he began to get bored, and looked around.

"This room must have been decorated by one of the best interior decorators of Paris. That's a lead I must follow. There aren't many of them, and there are also very few gorgeous blondes. Now it's simply child's play to find out who she is. But what the devil is this. Am I supposed to find out for myself who she is, or are those articles brought together for some other purpose? They surely don't belong in a boarding school for girls! This here must be Venus. She is making love to Mars. But I have never seen a statue like this. There is another nymph, or goddess, helping her! Poor Mars. And this statue is almost remarkably alive. The goddess seems to be secretly in love with herself, contemplating her own voluptuous charms. And this one! Oh, oh! That has nothing to do with classical mythology. She is beautiful and alone. But she does not seem to mind because she is very busy making love to herself. Priestess and victim at the same time? It's terrible, my dear little girl, to do these beautiful things all by your lonely self. You should ask some nice little boy to help you. But to look at the face of this little girl, it seems that the sculptor caught her at the right moment. An expression like that means only one thing. She's coming! God, I wish I had been that happy sculptor! Lady Evergreen has quite a collection. It seems to me that this daughter of Eve ignores the Laws of Moses. At least it does not seem to me that she is overly concerned about the terrible punishments with which the good Lord threatens those who eat of the forbidden fruit. There is another lady, in an almost life-size painting who is having her cunt treated in such a way as procreation surely never intended. Well, anyhow, she has an accomplice who seems to enjoy it tremendously. The woman is very beautiful, and the way she has her white thighs clamped around the neck of her lover, it almost makes me horny to look at it. Come on, my dear boy, stretch out your lecherous tongue a little bit farther. I know out of experience that the job is very demanding. But it's also terribly exciting, and you can be assured of great rewards. The expression of utter abandon and happiness on this woman's face is a work of art. I wonder who the painter is. That man isn't very good looking. Come to think of it, only the women in this curious collection are delectable and beautiful. I wonder if Lady Evergreen is about ready to receive me."

During this monologue, Maxim had investigated and admired every statuette, painting and etching. He now walked back to the couch and began to leaf through an album which was put on one of the little end tables. It was filled with erotic pictures. However, every single one of them portrayed lesbian scenes. He began to think.

"Now what," he asked himself, "would be the purpose of this long waiting, and this homosexual exhibition. Why am I supposed to sit among undoubtedly the most expensive collection of lesbian curiosa in all of Paris?"

And suddenly, in a flash, it came to him. He was leafing through an album with exquisite engravings. There was a couple, engaged in about every position of lovemaking one could think of. Only one position was missing. The one in which a man could get a woman with child!

And under the last engraving, written in a woman's style, it said, "Surely there are enough possibilities to express one's love, and to reach the highest peaks of ecstasy without using that one."

"Only a real ass needs more explanation," Count de Berny said to himself, "and I surely must have been one during our first encounter. At least, I am pleased that she credits me with common sense. She did invite me again. But dammit, how could I know what she expected from me. She looked so innocent and virginal. That goes to show you how easily one can be deceived by beautiful large blue eyes. My lady fair seems to be a true and accomplished priestess of Venus, and I may have to learn things I haven't even heard about yet!"

Dorothy interrupted his monologue. "Would your lordship be so kind as to follow me?"

And Maxim entered the room where he had spent so many beautiful hours just a few days ago. The room had not changed—it had the same chestnut-brown tapestries with pink flowers. Evergreen was stretched upon a sofa and she wore a negligée which seemed to go with her name. The folds of the transparent gown showed a chemise made mainly out of billows of lace and silk. Her negligée was embroidered with ruby-colored butterflies.

Flowers adorned her hair, and a large, exotic orchid was pinned on her breast, hiding part of her cleavage. Everything she wore was in perfect harmony with her soft com-

107

plexion. It was a pity that she covered her face with a mask.

"Oh, you evil little one," Maxim said while he took a deep breath after the long kiss they exchanged upon greeting, "I have waited so long for this moment. Three whole days without any thought other than whether or not I would ever see my darling Evergreen again. I don't know if I can forgive you!"

"Have you really thought so much about me? I am glad to hear that, and I am also glad to know that this serious occupation has not caused you to neglect to court a young lady from the chorus line at the Opéra, and to have a rendezvous with a well-known courtesan behind the discreet curtains of a certain famous restaurant in Paris."

"How do you know all these things? But let me assure you that . . ."

"My dearest Maxim, you do not have to find excuses. I am not the jealous type. I only mentioned it to let you know that I am not one of those empty-headed creatures who will do anything just to hear a well-turned phrase from their lover's mouth, and who believe everything he says. I know precisely when a man speaks, what he says and why he says it."

"Do you mean that we were at the Opéra and that restaurant at the same time—without me knowing about it?"

"Dearest, don't you know that love is blind?"

"Please, I am serious. Were you really there?"

"I did not say that!"

"But in the meantime . . ."

"In the meantime I notice that your passion has not yet reached the point where your instincts take over."

"I would not say that. My instincts are sharp enough to discover that you are the most gorgeous Evergreen I have ever seen. Your gown, my dearest, is the most elegant, because of its simplicity, the most comfortable because of its ease to wear, and—I guess—to take off. Your room is exquisite. The tapestries where roses and evergreens mix on a background of shimmering chestnut are the most beautiful I have ever seen, and . . ."

"Aha, I see that you keep your eyes open in the rooms where you go."

"Oh, there are certain little things that usually do not escape my attention when I am waiting in a room."

"Is that so?"

"Yes, and if you like the idea, I can prove to you that I have an excellent memory."

"That is not a bad idea at all, my dear friend." Evergreen got up from her sofa and, embraced by her lover, walked into the other room.

"For instance," the young man said, "this huge mirror was not here the last time I was in this sanctuary of love and beauty."

"Oh, yes, it was!"

"My dear little Evergreen, I am sure it was not."

"No, no, I assure you that it was here. Felicitas had forgotten to place it properly."

"I see. And the proper place is exactly opposite your bed, right?"

"Of course," Florentine answered, slightly blushing.

"I agree with you wholeheartedly, darling.

Is the glass of good quality, and are its reflections true to nature?"

"Why don't you see for yourself?"

"One minute, darling."

During this conversation, Maxim's hands had not been idle, and—straying through the billows of lace and silk—had soon discovered that his paramour's gown was only held together by a few ribbons. He quickly loosened them.

And the mirror was really a good one. It showed, when the billows of embroidered silk and lace slowly dropped to the floor, a perfect woman's body. Long, blonde hairs flowed down snow-white, well rounded shoulders. A patch of golden fleece covered an enchanting little love grotto. Maxim, who wanted to show that he was not a novice in the art of love, and who had been shown more than convincingly the extent of Lady Evergreen's passion, began to cover the wonderful breasts of the young woman with passionate, hot kisses. The little buds stretched voluptuously when his lips brushed past them and stretched more yearningly when he rolled them between his fingers. He tongued her breasts, caressed them with feverish hands, and did not forget the blonde tufts under her armpits.

Florentine let him do as he pleased; her eyes did not stray from the mirror for a single second. Intently, she followed every one of Maxim's movements.

He had picked her up and stretched her across the bed—Florentine anticipated all his movements. Staring at the mirror, she slowly spread her thighs, awaiting things to come with pounding heart and high expectations.

110

Maxim knelt down upon the bear rug in front of the bed. His loving fingers parted the silken curls of her quim, kissing the clitoris which he had bared. He kissed it, his eager tongue lapping across it, and it began to stretch and grow under his caresses till it was stiff enough for him to suck. He rolled it between his lips, and at the same time his hands eagerly twirled the nipples and kneaded the jutting breasts. The young woman sighed with a deep satisfaction.

"Aaah . . . it feels so good . . . oh, please, go on . . ."

"I was right," Maxim thought, "there was good reason for her to show me all those lesbian scenes."

"Oooh . . . it's delicious . . . how marvelous . . ." Lady Evergreen became more and more rapturous. ". . . please, not too quickly . . . I wish it to last forever and ever! Aaaah . . . ooh . . . please, please, darling lover . . . your tongue . . . I feel it . . . and your teeth . . . please, bite me tenderly!"

Maxim obeyed. He pressed his lips lovingly upon this downy peach which tasted better than anything he had ever tasted. He did not spend all his energy on the stiffened clitoris. After all, his love was no longer a young girl and he rightly suspected that the other parts of her vagina had also become sensitive enough to give her the greatest pleasure. His tongue strayed farther and his fingers took over the task of playing with the jumping clitoris. Florentine was floating in ecstasy. This was superior to Julia's kisses and caresses.

"Oh, my God . . . my dear God," she exclaimed, "if you keep this up I am afraid that

I can't . . . I can't . . . Oh, God . . . don't you hear me . . . I don't have the strength . . . I can't . . . it is impossible . . . Maxim . . . darling . . . it . . . oooh . . . I . . ."

Florentine's peach-blonde quim flooded, her marvelous body spasmed and jerked, and with a deep sigh she fell back into the pillows. She wanted to get up because she knew that she had been understood, but two strong hands pressed her back upon the bed. Maxim had begun to enjoy his task, and he wanted to see if he could cause her to have another orgasm.

He buried his head deeply between her thighs, his tongue fervently licking the insides of her sheath, his teeth nibbling sharply on her clitoris. With his index finger he slowly penetrated her tiny little asshole, while his thumb moved upwards to join his tongue. His prickly moustache mixed with the silken hairs of the moistened cunny and Florentine began to squirm and groan.

"Oooh," she suddenly exclaimed in a high-pitched voice, "I think I'm dying . . . I can't stand it.!" Maxim doubled his efforts and was soon rewarded by a copious flood which seemed to be drawn from her entire body, concentrating in her cunt. With his last effort, Maxim received the entire soul of this beautiful little blonde who fell back on the bed in a dead faint, without bothering to find out if her companion had also experienced a climax.

Maxim was tempted but, despite his extreme excitement, he managed to control himself, and he did not rape his paramour. He thought, "She obviously prefers going down over any other way of having sex, and I can't imagine that she will be so cold-blooded as not to repay me in at least a similar way."

And, he was right. When Florentine had recuperated enough from her ecstasy she sat up in the bed, threw her arms around Maxim's neck, and kissed him long and passionately.

"Oh, my lover, I love you so much. You have made me happier than I have ever been."

Her mouth drank his hot breath and her nimble fingers began to unbutton his clothes. When he, too, was completely naked, she rubbed her little nose against his rough skin and mixed in those caresses which brought new life to the hopes of the Count de Berny. She quickly slid down from the bed and pressed him backwards, returning all the delights she had received from him. Her lips trailed the hair on his chest, her tongue tipped down toward his navel, went lower, and she slowly kissed the tip of his prick. Her tongue flickered and sipped at his balls, and her sharp little teeth nibbled sweetly at the shaft of his throbbing tool. Though the young man was inexperienced in these things—he had always taken the lead immediately—and therefore a little bit shy, her ministrations brought him to the point of utmost excitement, but still he could not let himself go.

Florentine became a little impatient and she called out, "Come on, my darling . . . I am longing for you! I want to taste your love juices . . . don't withhold them from me. Quickly, give me your tool!"

The girl slipped her panting lips over the spongy head of his throbbing rod and clung tightly to it. The wealth of her scented blonde hair spilled across Maxim's belly. She also

113

clung to his balls with her fingers, and she took the entire length of his tool so far into her, so far past lips, teeth and tongue, deep into the velvety reaches of her throat, that Maxim feared she would strangle herself on so much meat. But Florentine knew what she was doing. She stroked the head softly into her palate, tenderly into her throat, creating a marvel of suction. The wet and drawing power seemed to pull all of Maxim into her mouth. He began to writhe and twist, and almost cried out loud for freedom. The explosive force was building up in his loins, aching in his belly, but every time he was about to come, Florentine switched the speed of her caresses, the tempo of her ministration and the rhythm of her sucking. Maxim's heaving tool responded to tongue and teeth as it throbbed manfully against the insides of her cheeks and the satiny depths of her throat. Florentine pulled upon his ramrod as if she wanted to pull his very backbone down through it.

Maxim grabbed her head and began to buck in a wild frenzy. Florentine followed all his movements in perfect counter-rhythm and she drew upon him with many gulpings and smackings. She drove him once again into the marvelous softness of her throat. It was too much.

Maxim let his semen fly in tremendous spurts. For the first time in his life not in a clinging quim but into the charming throat of his Lady Evergreen who ate so adoringly of his prick and who caressed his balls so sensually.

He fell back in near stupor, lying supine for quite some time. He was sweaty and had slick places between his legs and in the hair of his chest. While he recuperated, Florentine washed him with lukewarm, scented water and dried him with warmed towels.

Finally they were able to get up, and sat down in the other room at a table which was laden with the choicest food. They both did great honor to their late supper.

"Do you know, my beauty, that you belong to those quiet waters that are so deep and dangerous?"

"Why?" the young woman asked innocently.

"Why? Because you, my dear masked lady, have taught me in one evening more than I could ever dream of, and I am afraid that from now on a simple coupling and the enjoyment of caressing beautiful legs is no longer enough for me. And that almost makes me feel sad!"

"Really? I don't understand . . ."

"Yes, you do! But . . . if you don't regret anything, then I can only be happy. Is there, however, any chance that we will ever do it . . . ah . . . the other way?"

"I do not want to give you a flat 'no' to that question, because that depends entirely upon the future. I do not want to sound egotistical, but the chances are slim. You see, this way there are very few consequences . . . for me."

"I see," Maxim said smilingly. "This way we will never have a chance to get a little heir. But tell me, my darling, if you want to continue seeing me, is there ever a chance that I will see you without your mask?"

"That is the one and only thing, Maxim, that you should not ask of me. I am afraid that we would never meet again."

"I don't insist upon it, darling Evergreen,

though I must admit that it is slightly embarrassing."

"Only a little bit!"

"Oh, you little dictator. Your will be done." And he bowed mockingly in her direction. "But tell me darling, who painted those voluptuous pictures in your little waiting room? And who was the sculptor? And who made those perfect etchings?"

"I have no idea. I told Felicitas what I wanted, and she saw to it that the room was decorated."

"Felicitas, the Negro woman?"

"Yes."

"I would love to own a similar collection."

"Maybe she is willing to help you." The answer was properly evasive.

"Oh, you suspicious creature. Are you afraid that I would try and uncover your identity through the painters and the sculptor? Be sure that one of these days it may happen. The Topinambours club is terribly upset that two of their members have had a secret rendezvous, and they have made up their minds that they are going to find out who the lady in question really is."

"Two rendezvous? I assure you, Maxim, that I have never . . ."

"I know, darling, because the other one is as dark as you are blonde. And this daughter of the land of Spain calls herself Pomegranate Flower. That nickname would never do for you, darling. But you cannot deny that you don't know about whom I am talking. Poor Count de Paliseul is terribly unhappy. He has heard not a single word from his sphinx for days; he has almost stopped eating and drinking."

"He does look a little bit depressed lately."

"Do you know him?"

"I have seen him riding in the Bois de Boulogne now and then," she evaded the question.

"The poor man. Can't you do anything for him? I am sure that his love must be a good friend of yours. Can't you put in a good word for him. Tell Lady Pomegranate Flower to have pity on him."

"I am sorry, I cannot do that. But if I were him, I would forget about the entire episode."

"What makes you say that?"

"Because I happen to know that the affair is over, and that he did not live up to Pomegranate's expectations."

"Does she have a waiting room like yours?"

"Not as far as I know. Moreover, it is not up to me to tell about her. I know that she would never talk about me. I am only doing your friend de Paliseul a favor, because neither you, nor he, nor your entire club will ever find out about our identities."

"My dearest Evergreen, how about going to bed together for a good night's rest?"

"Oh, no, my friend. It is too late, and I would miss the last train."

"What? You are leaving in the middle of the night?"

"Yes."

"Do you live far away from Paris?"

"I live in Paris, in Rome, in Chicago, in Timbuktu. Darling, don't try to find out."

"You are right, my love. I don't like it, but

I am afraid that I have to live with it. When shall I see you again?"

"In about a week."

"Oh, please, darling, can't you be more specific. I hate to share the fate of my poor friend de Paliseul."

"You don't have to worry, and to prove it to you, expect a message for Thursday."

"It's a date! Thursday then!" Maxim kissed his lovely lady, Florentine pulled the bell cord and Felicitas promptly appeared. De Berny was now more than ever intent upon finding out his love's identity.

"Dear Miss Felicitas," he said, pressing five gold pieces in her hand, "would you do me the favor of telling me where I can buy an album with etchings like the one I leafed through in Madame's little waiting room?"

"I am sorry, my lord, I can't," Felicitas answered. "But I will be more than happy to get you one. And it is not necessary to pay me in advance. His Lordship is one of those gentlemen whose credit is good, and I am one of those servants who do not betray their mistresses."

Maxim put the money which she handed him back in his purse, and he entered the equipage with Felicitas. After, it seemed, he had crisscrossed half of Paris, the coach stopped, he got out, and—much to his surprise —he was standing in front of the Club de Topinambours. The equipage was speeding away in the direction of the Champs Elysées.

Somebody tapped on his shoulders. It was de Paliseul and a priest.

"I see you had a date again?"

"Yes, I had a wonderful time."

"Did you find out who she was?"

"No, and I don't think I will try!"

"I have told our fellow members that I will warn them as soon as I get my invitation. They will follow at a discreet distance, and then we will know who our paramours are."

"I am afraid I have a sad message for you, my friend. It seems that your Pomegranate Flower was not pleased with your . . . ah . . . performance . . ." Maxim threw a glance in the direction of the priest.

"Excuse me," de Paliseul said, "this is Father Lang from London. I was going to see to it that he could stay at my housekeeper's during his vacation in Paris. Unfortunately, she was indisposed. I have told him about our adventures. You do not have to keep secrets from him. And what do you mean, she was not pleased with my performance?" His face flushed red.

"I am sorry, my friend. I am merely a messenger, and I have been told by Lady Evergreen who is a very good friend of your lady love, to convey this message. It seems that the ladies know exactly what we are doing and what we are thinking. I have tried to unravel the secret and I have been very unsuccessful. One thing, though—I am not going to endanger any future dates by prying into their secrets. After all, I have given my word of honor."

De Paliseul was terribly upset. Maxim told him to go into the club and get good and drunk. He offered to take Father Lang to the home of his own housekeeper, the widow Lemaitre who, he was sure, would be more than happy to have a border.

Father Lang was as pleased as de Paliseul was unhappy. He assured de Paliseul that he

could fully understand the young man's feelings, thanked him for all the trouble he had
gone through in his behalf, and he told Maxim
that he was very grateful for helping a poor,
stranded priest in the big city.

Maxim hailed a cab, and de Paliseul went
poutingly into the Club de Topinambours. De
Berny and Father Lang were soon on their way
to the simple home of the widow Lemaitre.

CHAPTER EIGHT

"Oh, your Reverence, it would be a great honor for me to have you as a guest in my humble home," gushed the widow Lemaitre, after Maxim had posed the question. She fluttered her eyelashes, and produced a charming blush which would have done honor to a girl in her teens.

"Since my poor husband died," she continued after Maxim de Berny had left, in the secure knowledge that the good priest would not be left untended, "I have had an empty room. It always saddens me each time I pass it, because it was in that very room that my dear Jean-Baptiste and I came together for the first time in wedded bliss. Alas!" She dried a tear and modestly blew her nose.

Father Lang was already smitten, especially since he had heard Maxim's entire story during the long ride in the cab. He quivered with eagerness to take possession of the bereaved widow Lemaitre. He knew, moreover, from Maxim that she had been a widow for quite some time and that she found solace with the boarders she took in on occasion.

"It is most generous of you, my daughter, and the Lord shall bless you for it," Father Lang said to her with an unctuous smile. "Here are ten francs for the first week and I hope that there will be enough left to purchase such little food as I may require."

"Oh, good Father, with so much money I can easily feed you on chicken and duckling every day," exclaimed the happy widow. "Let me show Your Reverence to his room. No man has entered it since my poor Jean-Baptiste found his eternal reward." And, realizing too late that she was talking to a priest she added hastily, "for which I daily pray, hoping that he has attained it by now."

The buxom widow went ahead of him, and his eyes fixed on the seductive swing of her magnificent broad hips, watching her truly remarkable backside which was encased in a skirt at least three sizes too tight for her. She was just the type he had hoped for.

Madame Lemaitre opened a narrow door, inclining her head as he entered. The furniture consisted of a low bed, a footstool, a chest of drawers and a short-backed chair. A little window stood at about shoulder height, and a motley bearskin—possibly thrown out by de Berny—was on the floor.

With a satisfied smile on his lips Father Lang said, "An excellent room, Madame. It has all the privacy one could wish for. I am truly grateful to you."

"But it is I who is grateful to you, Father. Ten francs. Oh! It's a bounty from heaven itself." She grabbed his hand and kissed it fervently.

He patted her benignly on the head with his free hand, saying, "You do me too much credit, my daughter. Money is but the stuff to be shared with those who are in need of it. And now, with your permission, I would like to retire to regain my strength."

"Certainly, your Reverence, certainly," the buxom widow Lemaitre cooed, her voice low and seductive. She curtsied when she left the room, giving Father Lang a splendid look into her cleavage as well as a hot desire for her speedy return. Then she closed the door behind her.

The Father unpacked his valise, put his few articles of clothing in the drawers and then, removing his cassock and little cornered hat, he stretched out on the bed, clad only in a pair of short underpants.

He closed his eyes and let out a sigh of content. He began to think about the stories he had heard from the Counts de Paliseul and de Berny, regretting that he no longer had the age and vigor of both gentlemen. But, unfortunately, there was the good widow Lemaitre and, unless his judgment was entirely wrong, he was sure that she longed to be possessed by him as much as he wanted to mount her. The mere thought of the endless possibilities awaiting him during his month's vacation made his crotch swell. It did not take very long before his virile cock was in a gigantic erection.

About fifteen minutes later there was a discreet tap on his door. In fact, it was so discreet that it could barely be heard. Father Lang therefore decided that it would be infinitely better to pretend having fallen asleep. His breathing was regular, his eyes were closed, and his massive organ stood up like a flagpole. The door opened very slowly till it was slightly ajar, and the head of the widow peeked around the corner. She did not hear a sound from her new lodger, other than his regular breathing and she opened the door a little wider, softly slipping through. She quietly tiptoed into the room.

At once she noticed the enormous erection of the priest. Her eyes widened and a deep flush covered her face. She came toward the

123

bed silently and, bending down to stare at this mighty symbol of manhood her lips formed a silent O of utter amazement. Just at that moment, Father Lang opened his eyes. He stared at her, asking with a low voice, "Is anything the matter, Madame Lemaitre?"

She hastily turned her stare away from his prick and stammered, "Oh . . . no . . . your Reverence. I . . . I . . . only wanted to ask what you might want to have for breakfast. I did not know . . . that I was going to have a border and I do not have very much in the larder for myself. I . . . I . . . wanted to go early to the market . . . to . . . to . . . prepare a few delicacies. I . . . I . . ." her eyes were irresistibly drawn back to the loins of the good Father, "wanted to ask your preference."

"I shall eat whatever you eat, Madame. Please, do not go to any trouble on my account, I pray you."

"As . . . as . . . your . . . Reverence wishes," stammered the widow, but she gave no sign of intention that she was about to leave his room. She was completely hypnotized by that huge tool which prodded against the thin material of his drawers to the bursting point.

He pillowed his head on his folded arms. "Is there anything else you want to ask me, my daughter?" he asked politely.

"N . . . n . . . no . . ." was all she could utter, yet her fists were clenched and her arms were drawn against her sides. Her huge bosom heaved with quick rising and falling motions, her eyes bulged and sweat broke out on her forehead. The blush had spread and her ears and the tip of her nose were almost fiery red.

Father Lang wanted to get her out of this

state of shock and he decided to make it a little bit easier on her. He gave her a long and meaningful look and then said calmly, as if he were discussing the weather, "You are staring at my cock, Madame, as if it were something unique. Let me assure you, dear woman that half the world's population has one. And, far be it from me to offend your modesty, but mine is frequently in this condition when I am resting. I would not want you to think that I intend any assault upon your undisputed virtue."

"Oooh . . . but . . . I . . . ah . . . did not . . . think that . . . at all," the blushing widow gasped. "I am sure that a priest would never take notice of such a lowly person as myself but, with your Reverence's permission, your c—cock is s—so s—swollen . . . that I . . . that I . . . could n—not help b—but notice it."

"Do not feel guilty, my daughter," was the mellow reply. "Your kindness in giving me shelter has put you high above any other woman in Paris. And I think that you are very comely, and cannot help but wonder that no honorable man has yet replaced your late husband."

Emilia Lemaitre lowered her head. "I . . . I have tried, Father. But I cannot find a man worthy to replace my dear Jean-Baptiste. Of course, God forgive his soul, he did have his faults, but . . ."

"We all have them, my daughter."

"Yes, your Reverence. I . . . I was going to mention that my poor Jean-Baptiste did not always share the bed with me as often as I wished. But . . . he was very much a man like you . . I mean . . ."

125

She turned aside. She was terribly embarrassed at the things she had blurted out, and she would have loved to run out of the room. But she had been completely under the spell of Father Lang's gigantic member. Fortunately, the good Father had seized her by the hand, and he encouraged her line of thought by saying, "I am not at all offended, my daughter. On the contrary, by comparing me to a husband who gave you heaven on earth, I feel very pleased and flattered. Marriages are made in heaven and it gladdens my heart to hear about couples who take satisfaction and joy in each other."

"Thank you, Father. It's only that . . . well, that . . . Jean-Baptiste did not always take his joy when it was offered. We often quarreled about that. And now I repent my sinfulness. I . . . I asked him to do things which he said were a disgrace in the eyes of the Lord, and he swore that they were absolutely forbidden, even between husband and wife. He began to drink, and he left my bed."

"Nothing that is done between husband and wife, when it is done in love, can be improper, my daughter. What a pity that he did not understand this law of God and Nature."

He prompted, "Will it ease your conscience to tell me about the nature of the difficulties between you and your late husband?"

"Oooh, your Reverence," she clasped her hands before her mouth, "I would not dare in a million years . . ."

"Come, come, my daughter. If I cannot measure the nature of the misunderstanding— because I am sure that it was nothing more—I can hardly help you alleviate your distress. I am on vacation from my order for an entire month. Look at me as a good friend, and try to forget that I am a priest." He almost added, "So will I," but he checked himself just in time.

She whispered, "You won't condemn me?"

"Of course not!"

He did not let go of her trembling hand and Madame Lemaitre suddenly blurted, "I sometimes wished that Jean-Baptiste would take me from behind in the way I had seen it done by the animals in the fields and he would always say that this was the most unnatural and horrible thing a respectable woman could wish for and . . ."

He stopped her gushing confession. "Following the example set by Nature, how could he take offense?"

The widow Emilia Lemaitre squirmed, turning her head away. She tried to draw her hand away from his, but Father Lang held on, insistently. "Disclose the secrets you are hiding in your mind. They trouble you because you don't talk about them. Out with them, and they will no longer be a source of distress to you."

"T—true . . . your . . . your . . . Reverence . . ." Emilia began to stutter hopelessly, "I—it w—was n—not only the, the, the t—taking me from behind . . . that m—my h—husband ob—objected to. It . . . is s—so d—difficult . . . to . . . to . . . tell a . . . a . . . priest."

"I cannot at all fathom your difficulties, my daughter, if you keep stuttering and stammering I want to be helpful, and I am sure that I can be very, very accommodating, because men of my calling are usually more informed and tolerant about the things of this world. And, as I have assured you before, pray see me as a good and understanding friend rather than a priest."

"I wished him to put his . . . prick . . . into . . . into . . . the other place, your Reverence!"

"The other place?" Father Lang pretended not to understand. "I think it would be better if you showed me. It is always so much more simple than groping for the proper words. Take off your skirts, my daughter, and I am sure that we will have no difficulty communicating. Point out that . . . other place to me."

His prick had attained its full length and girth. Emilia Lemaitre drew a long, trembling breath, she unhooked her skirt, letting it drop about her shapely ankles. She wore nothing under it, and the good father nearly swooned when he saw the soft curves of her pink-skinned belly, marked by a wide and shallow navel niche and then below a thicket of dark pubic curls which in a huge fleece covered the opening of her delicious slit. But before he could compliment her on her good looks she had turned her back, pointing her forefinger toward the narrow, shadowy cleft which separated her two magnificently ripe, fully rounded globes. She whispered huskily, "It was in here, Father, that I wanted Jean-Baptiste to put his cock. But he said that it was wicked to do that. I begged him to do it only to show me that he truly loved me. I always was willing, eager for him to fuck me the regular way. But he always refused to grant me the one pleasure I wanted more than anything in the world."

Father Lang could no longer contain himself. The widow's beautiful buttocks were making him exceedingly horny and he stretched out both hands, firmly squeezing and kneading the delicious globes. Emilia was startled and she looked around, her eyebrows raised in utter surprise. In a last effort to retain her modesty, she clasped both hands before her big fleece.

"Jean-Baptiste was wrong to deny you your greatest desire," purred the priest, "especially since you did your utmost to make his husbandly rights memorable. He mercilessly denied you a token of his husbandly affection."

"Oh, that's so true," the beautiful half-naked widow sniffed, taking her hands off her furry slit to rub two big tears from her eyes.

"Do you still want these things, my child? Do you like to be buggered?"

A ripple of voluptuous desire shivered through the body of Emilia Lemaitre. Her voice was husky and faint as she whispered,

"Oh yes, oh yes, oh yes."

"I shall be more than happy to help you in your time of need, my dear child. Would it offend you, if I fucked you in the ass?"

"Oh no . . . no!"

"Then allow me a little preparation, dear daughter. Lie across my lap." She did not comprehend his instructions at all, but she would gladly have done anything to deserve this unexpected boon for which she had been yearning those many, many years. She complied, though blushingly, and the priest circled her waist with his left arm, raising his right hand. She did not know what was about to happen and when Father Lang dealt her a loud slap on the huge summit of one of her bottom cheeks, leaving a bright mark, she was startled and fearful.

"Ooh," she gasped, undoubtedly trying to

figure out how this punishment was going to lead to the sodomitic bliss she was yearing for.

"Don't move," he ordered, dealing her a second slap on the other buttock, leaving another handmark on her velvety skin. "This will warm your backside, arouse your desires and therefore prepare you to enjoy what otherwise might easily become an ordeal."

Emilia was satisfied with the explanation, so she bravely clenched her fists and closed her eyes, submitting to this strange preparation. Her naked loins wriggled voluptuously over Father Lang's enormously bulging crotch, putting his powers of self-control to the test. But manfully he continued to slap her succulent rump till it was dark red. The helpless victim wriggled, sobbed and kicked in the most exciting manner.

"I do believe that you are now properly prepared for the gratification of your secret desires." He tried to keep his voice unctuous and fatherly, but this was a miserable failure. Instead, his voice shook, was hoarse and thick with unbridled lust.

"Take off the rest of your clothes and get up upon the bed on all fours," he commanded. "Spread your legs far apart; it will make it easier for me to get in."

Slowly, rubbing her flaming buttocks, Emilia clambered from his lap. She took off her blouse and bodice, and naked as the day she was born she got up onto the bed. Her head was bowed, her palms bore down upon the mattress, and her knees were wide apart. The spectacle of her thoroughly paddled bottom made his mouth water, his cock throb, and his head spin. The contrast of her pink thighs and calves was a delight to behold.

Father Lang removed his drawers, giving his massive prick full freedom. He massaged her red buttocks with expert fingers, and the beautiful Emilia whimpered with lust. Finally he pried in between the cleft, exposing the crinkly little asshole. The dainty lips contracted with becoming modesty, a movement which only served to make Father Lang more horny —to judge by the almost painful throbs of his cock. He kept the globes separated with the fingers of his left hand and he slowly stuck his index finger of the right hand into the inviting little rosette. He caressed it, making Emilia moan and sigh incoherently. Finally he gently introduced the tip of his prick into the narrowness of the entrance to her bowels.

"Oooh . . . your Reverence," she gasped, her hips jerking fitfully at his furtive probings.

"Patience, patience, my dear daughter," he said. "I am fully able to satisfy your heart's desire, but I must have your full cooperation. I can guarantee you the results you have been praying for."

He slowly withdrew his forefinger out of the widow's cringing ass, and spreading the buttocks wide apart, began to moisten the crinkly hole with his lecherous tongue till the center of the cleft was dripping with his spittle. She weaved and undulated her hips in the most lascivious manner. Father Lang spit in his hand and then rubbed the saliva on the tip of his turgid cock.

After he had thoroughly moistened his entire instrument so that it was properly slippery, he said, "Now, my daughter, we shall have to

131

see about the respective measurements. Please, try and stay calm when you feel me penetrate these tight inroads into your pleasure spot. If you retreat, the good work will have to be repeated."

"Oooh . . . no . . . no, your Reverence!" Emilia's naked body shook and convulsed with erotic fervor.

Now he put both hands to work against the quivering buttocks of her reddened backside, making them yawn widely till the dainty niche was lewdly distended, gaping in readiness for his adventure. He fitted the big head of his stiff organ against the little opening, and edged forward with a few tentative pushes. The lips gave way to his superior strength, but it seemed that they were only capable of accepting the knob of his formidable cock. A low groan escaped from the lips of his landlady who dug her fingers deep into the mattress, butting her head against the counterpane of the bed to steel herself against the oncoming assault.

"And now to the good work," he gasped, thrusting vigorously. The good widow Lemaitre ground her teeth, but she met the onslaught with heroic resistance. The priestly prick penetrated slowly into the narrow channel. He noticed at once that his dear Emilia surely could not be a virgin in that crevice, though she was almost as tight as a virgin. This little circumstance doubled the enjoyment of Father Lang's carnal pleasure in servicing her. By now, more than an inch of his hot and turgid rod had disappeared into her warm, narrow cavern. Convulsions made her buttocks quake and shiver. He held on firmly to her big fat arse, spreading the cheeks as widely as he could, at the

132

same time making sure that Emilia would not try to escape that which she had so boldly sought.

"Brace yourself again, my daughter. I am going to return to the task of making you happy," he panted. He jerked his loins again, sending his cock deeper into her rectum. A muffled cry escaped her lips. Father Lang's cock was now buried halfway into the hot chamber of her bowel. He stopped. The rudely distended passageway clutched spasmodically against his shuddering organ in a series of quick pressures. He had to use all his powers of self-control, or he would have spurted all his spunk.

"Am I hurting you, my daughter?" His voice again was unctuous, though it still trembled somewhat.

"Oooh . . . your Reverence," Emilia squirmed, "it . . . it is all I can bear. I have never before been stretched so terribly . . . aaaah . . . ooooh . . . please, I beg of you, wait a moment so that I can regain my strength. I want to have all of you inside me."

"Bravely spoken, my dear . . . ah . . . child," he panted. "I, too, need some respite. Try to bow your head a little lower against the bedboard. It will angle up your bottom and make my thrusting inside you all the more delightful."

She immediately complied with his request. Her thighs began to quake, threatening to give way beneath her in near-fainting ecstasy. The priest slowly crouched forward, extending his left hand under her to grope for her enormous tits which he began to squeeze lovingly. With his other hand he crawled around her furry patch, trying to find her clitoris. When he had found it, he began to squeeze it gently. Emilia emitted a sobbing cry of pure ecstasy, "Aiii . . . ooohh . . . you are making me die with pleasure. I swear to you no one ever has made me so happy . . . not even my dear Jean-Baptiste. Oh, dear Lord . . . I will burn a candle for my dear departed husband, for the good Count de Berny who brought me to you, and for this heavenly evening!"

"Amen to that, my hospitable daughter," Father Lang rapturously agreed. "And now that I have regained my full composure, prepare yourself to feel my blade disappear up to the hilt into that marvelous chink of yours!"

"Oh, I am ready! I enjoy it, even though it may kill me," exclaimed his eager landlady.

The Englishman gritted his teeth, thrusting manfully forward. He tried to distract his naked victim by squeezing her tits and frigging her hardening clit. Emilia Lemaitre was now writhing lasciviously upon the bed, uttering sobbing little cries of joy and ecstasy, and thrusting back her naked hips wildly so that the priest might harpoon her fundament to his very hilt, as he had promised.

Father Lang felt the shuddering, wriggling buttocks thrust against his naked belly. His face turned purple in a desperate effort not to squirt his jism into her yet. His finger twisted Emilia's turgid clitoris, bringing her responses to a furious frenzy. Her fingers clawed the mattress, her head—no longer resting against the headboard—was shaking furiously and he could feel the naked tit jut and rasp its swollen nipple against the palm of his cupping hand.

Now he began to work his mighty weapon in and out of her protesting channel which was

134

spasming and contracting. The naked widow squirmed and twisted, seemingly trying to disengage herself from the tormenting spear. But her sobbing cries implied otherwise.

"Oooooh . . . aaah . . . faster . . . harder . . . your Reverence, please! Your finger is driving me out of my mind . . . oooh . . . oooh . . . don't come now, Reverend Father . . . please, please hold it back till I am ready, too! Deeper, harder . . . give it to me . . . drill as far as it will go . . . I beg of you! Oooh, what bliss, what joy you give me . . . aaah!!!"

His forefinger flattened the clitoris back into its dainty little abode. Then he let it bob up again in all its rigidity, rubbing it from side to side. Then he would press it down, only to let it jump up again. He drew her closer and closer towards that abyss of passion into which the hot, tight, squeezing glove of her rectal entrance against his embedded prick threatened to plunge him at any moment.

Finally, because of her quaking spasms and the tireless wriggling of her smooth, naked hips, he decided that she too had reached the point of no return. He called out to her to go with him on his flight into heaven and with two or three more tearing digs of his bursting weapon, he flooded her bowels with enormous squirts of hot, sticky jism. Her own furry slit offered its creamy sacrifice into his hands and Emilia Lemaitre's arms and legs gave way beneath her. She was sprawled flat, full-length upon the bed with the good Father closely joined to her ass. They both gasped out their ecstasy.

And thus, a visiting English priest had a most marvelous night because Julia de Corriero decided never to see the Count de Paliseul

again, and because her sister, the widow Vaudrez, did not trust the Count de Berny enough
for a stay overnight, fearing the noble gentleman could get her with child.

Strange are the ways of the Lord. Father
Lang took up his new domicile for the month
and at the same time he satisfied the secretive
burning desire of the frustrated, stately widow
of the late Jean-Baptiste Lemaitre.

CHAPTER NINE

"Well, my dear sister," Florentine asked Julia after breakfast, "what happened last night? Why did I have to go so quickly to Paris?"

"Because I had quite an unexpected adventure." Julia was radiant. She told her sister in detail what had happened, and she also mentioned that she had promised to visit Michael in his studio.

"You better be very careful, dear. This Mister Michael has seen you without a mask, and undoubtedly he would recognize you instantly!"

"Oh, I don't think that he moves around in our circles. I don't for one instant deny that you are right, but somehow I feel compelled to see this adventure through to the very end. This Michael Lompret is original and natural and I am irresistibly drawn to him. His language is different, his ideas are new and fresh, and love to him is so natural and uncomplicated. I am not in love with him, not yet. But my thoughts have been constantly with him. In fact, I have not thought about anything or anybody else."

"Aha! You are that far gone already!" Madame Vaudrez smilingly wagged her finger.

"Oh, no! Don't be silly," Julia answered, somewhat irritated. And, changing the subject quickly, "What have you and Maxim been doing?"

"Darling, I have discovered a whole new world. I have lived on an island of indescribable happiness!"

"Oh? Could you be a little bit more specific, please? What did you do on that island?"

"Oh, well, actually nothing in particular. I mean, we did not do anything that you had not already taught me, but it was more refined and —I don't know precisely how to say this—it got me infinitely more excited. The moustache and his squirting, it all made a big difference. You see, when a man knows how to make love in the same way women can love one another, there are certain advantages."

"In other words, I have been dethroned?"

"Oh, no . . . darling! How could you say that!"

"Sister dear, as far as my personal preferences go, I will never beg you for the pleasure. I am not so fond of these refinements as you are. I simply don't have the time to slowly enjoy these voluptuous pleasures. My blood boils too quickly when I am being caressed by an expert. And then I want to feel it deep inside me. That eternal knocking and slurping at the front door would drive me insane, because it gives me no deep ecstasy. One of these days, dear Florentine, I want to meet a man who is fully compatible in body and soul. And when that day arrives, I'll be the happiest woman in the world."

"And for that you would really drop your mask?"

"I really don't know what I would do. But it seems to me that your mask is an obstacle to your ultimate pleasures in lovemaking."

"It was in the way just a little bit."

"You better watch out, sister dear."

"You don't have to worry, Mrs. Careful. But what about your Michelangelo? Don't you

138

think you should have him checked out by Dorothy?"

"Oh, no," Julia said, "I don't want anybody to meddle in this romance. It would destroy the freshness, the naturalness of our affair. I want to find out if I can find happiness with this man!"

Her dark eyes sparkled, and Florentine, who knew the danger signs of her sister's outbursts, began to laugh.

"Come, come, Julia," she reprimanded, "don't get so upset. I'll take Cherub into the park and play with him for awhile. Why don't you lie down and quiet your nerves. Then we can talk all afternoon."

But Julia was not in the mood for any talking. She wanted to be in the arms of Michael Lompret. She was also disappointed to hear that her sister continued her lesbian practices, even though it was with a man. She wished that she had never introduced her sister to muffdiving and cocksucking. She therefore said, "No, dear, I have a lot to do tomorrow. I think it is better for me to return to Paris."

*　*　*

Julia was not the only one that day who was walking around slightly frustrated, and looking for a way to remove the emptiness that clutched at her heart. Maxim de Berny had lived through one of the most voluptuous nights he had ever spent in his entire young officer's life. But nevertheless, something was lacking. He adored his unknown Lady Evergreen, and he had no intention of giving her up. He definitely would show up whenever the sphinx summoned him. But he deemed it only proper to

139

find another outlet for his desires to compensate for those things which his secretive paramour might deny him forever.

He walked down the district where the courtesans lived, looking for a pick-up who might restore his feeling of manliness. "Yes," he thought, "that's it. I am the man! Not a partner in a silly lesbian affair! I admit that it was delicious, but even Lady Evergreen is not going to emasculate me. One of these days I shall teach her what a good fuck really is." His pace quickened as he walked through the district.

The girl was young and fair. If it had not been her profession, she would have gladly taken this young, blond officer into her home for free. Now all she could do to show her appreciation to him for having selected her, was to take off her clothes as quickly as possible. She wished she did not have to remember the feel of her quim from her previous customer, but there was nothing a girl could do about the ways she chose to make an honest living.

Maxim was kissing her neck, sucking up the young, tender flesh. His hands were roving down her spine, stroking her buttocks, caressing her shoulders, reaching under the buttocks, cupping them and pulling them up and in toward him. This was a man she'd always dreamed about. She tensed her thighs, sighed a deep sigh of passion and gave herself to their union.

Maxim's fingers seemed to burn as they coursed gently over her flesh. He kept imagining that he was doing these things to Lady Evergreen, and his passion became even greater. His gentle fingers tasted her softness and roundness, the glossy texture of her smooth

140

skin, her warm and responsive trembling. Her body rubbed and squirmed against his and he dug his fingers deep into her, grabbing the flesh in a handful until she squealed.

He lifted her and carried her to the bed. He stood over her, reaching down, catching her breasts. He eased them up toward him, elongating them with his hands. He knelt beside her and bending over, kissed her fiercely, invading her mouth with his insisting tongue. He pulled his mouth suckingly from hers, catching a small, pink nipple between his teeth. He sucked at her breasts, drawing as much of the solid flesh in his mouth as he could. Her nipples hardened and she gasped loudly. She took his hand and put it on the furry triangle that covered her slit.

Still kneeling, he moved down the bed and raised her thighs, spreading them wide. Her pale blue eyes watched him with a deep look of concentrated passion. Could this be how the eyes of Lady Evergreen would look if it weren't for that damned mask?

"Kiss me," she begged.

He looked down where the pink flesh of her cunt was open and then he slithered down, putting his lips to it. Yes, he had had a good taskmaster! She gave a surprised little shriek as she felt his sucking pressure. He began to suck the moist, rain-tasting flesh. He poked his tongue as high as it would go, moving around the walls of her sheath. He licked the insides of her hot thighs, then found and seized in his lips the hardening clitoris.

The girl had flung her thighs wide and was wriggling and shrieking with tiny, helpless explosions every second. Her fists clenched and unclenched beside her head on the bed. Her face was drawn in harrowed passion, swinging from side to side with jerky, involuntary movements. Maxim buried his face deep between her thighs, cupping his hands under her taut buttocks, levering them up.

"Oh, oh, oh, oooooh!!"

Her gasping moans assailed his ears, her moist, warm slipperiness drove him to a frenzy. His prick had become heavy, too heavy, and he needed to throw off his load. But when he drew his mouth away, she tried to catch at his head, pleading desperately with him not to stop now. He bent back to her and her loins leapt up to meet him. Her mouth was emitting a long, drawn out, continuous whine. This was a woman he possessed, rather than a woman who possessed him. He could sense her whole body twisting and turning in ecstatic torment. He wanted to get into her, but the fury of her excitement was at this point more fascinating to him than ramming it in and fucking her.

He heard her gasp. She shuddered and reached a long, drawn out climax. She continued to writhe and moan and he continued to kiss and lick her gently, bringing her back to a second intensity of passion. Maxim came away from her loins then, and moved up her body, tracing its light bulges with his lips. He knelt astride her, and she reached down, taking his rigid, pulsating penis which stuck out horizontally between her breasts.

She put it between her marvelous titties, pushing them up into a ravine of cleavage and for several moments he was rubbing up and down between the warm, firm flesh of her breasts. He felt a tingling deep in his loins and he moved forward on her again.

She reached up, her eyes sparkling with lust, and took his prick in both hands. He leaned forward on his hands and she covered the flaming knob with her lips. She took it into her mouth and he felt, with streaks of fire, her tongue licking and nuzzling the passion point of his knob.

She began to suck as she licked, sucking on the rest of his rigidity, biting gently on the shaft from time to time. Her eyes watched him—those beautiful blue eyes! He held her face with his hands, guiding it, feeling her cheeks hollowing rhythmically around the long length of flesh which filled her mouth.

"Harder," he gasped.

He felt her answering response and he began to rock slightly. She had released his prick with her hands and was stroking his muscular buttocks with them. She was breathing heavily, passionately, through her flared nostrils and he could feel her hips moving again under him. Her hands couldn't stay still on him and he felt them, suddenly, drawing lines of loin-convulsing sensation across and around his balls which hung down against her breasts.

He gasped aloud at the new attack and shoved his prick into her mouth so hard that for a moment she had to fight for breath.

He pulled his throbbing prick out of her mouth and moved down. He took her by the ankles and lifted her legs, spreading them as they rose. He bent her legs way back, whispering, "Oooh, those legs, those beautiful legs . . . now I am going to possess those beautiful legs and I am going to fuck the delicious little

143

cunt in between them! Ooh, my dear, dear Evergreen, finally I am going to fuck that delicious cunt between your legs."

She hooked her slender legs over his shoulders, his hips went ahead and his prick drove deeply into her young, quivering body.

He pushed his muscular shoulders forward, hands cupping her strongly. Lifting her, he gained deeper entrance. She began to moan, her hips began writhing, moving ahead then back, then twisting before rising again, hard and solid against his hips.

All the while he murmured, "Oooh . . . Evergreen . . . Evergreen . . . I am holding your legs, your beautiful legs . . . I am the Master . . . I want your cunt!"

She was oblivious of his chattering. "Oh-oh-oh-oh-oh," she cried out in a staccato chatter of gasps.

His knob felt the softness of flesh high up in her belly. The walls of her cunt were tight and warm, but moistly prepared against the huge expansion of his desire-bloated prick.

Pantingly he drove up into her with all the pressure he could muster. It seemed as if his passion began all the way down in his toes. His belly flopped against her crotch and his hairs mingled wetly with hers. His prick crushed up into her so hard that it brought a spasm of pain into her joy. She groaned in an orgy of passion. Her hanging, floating tongue in his mouth had now become the symbol of his complete mastery over her. She had given herself to him to do as he wished. He could hurt her, give her pain, pleasure, take her body and twist her soul.

Again he crashed heavily down on top of

144

her and she twisted in ecstatic fury under him, as if she wanted him to pierce her through, right up to the neck.

He straightened up from her, leaning at an angle, pulling her behind off the bed so that her hips were the highest point of her body. He crashed in and in and up and up, tearing her moist flesh with his great rifling cannon.

He felt her scream rather than heard it. His prick seemed loaded down with the weight of thunder. The thunder was preparing to burst. Relief was coming.

"Now . . . now . . ." he barked a command, and he could hear her answering gasps.

The thunder grew into a great cloud which suddenly burst. The liquid hot rain burst through and up into her belly as she screamed and jackknifed her legs up and down several times.

*   *   *

Madame de Corriero's heart was pounding rapidly when she made plans to escape the solicitous eyes of her devoted Dorothy. The maid had laid out a simple, pearl-gray travel costume the other day and knew therefore that her mistress was planning a trip.

But Julia's plan for deception was as simple as it was effective. She had ordered her coachman to drive her to the station, and to be sure to avoid suspicion, her maid had bought a ticket to one of the outlying towns. She ordered the coachman to pick her up at a certain time, and walked inside the big hall. Once she was sure that her servants had disappeared, she simply hailed a cab, and gave him the address of Michael Lompret.

Michael's door opened promptly when the cab drove up. An elderly servant stood at the opening and said, "Would Madame be so kind as to go inside. I will take care of the coachman." The old man—his name was Jonathan —had carefully looked Julia over, and his gaze was one of complete approval.

Two open arms awaited Julia when she entered the artist's studio and her first thought was that this was a rather expensive home for an artist. The cottage-type house, and the fact that Michael had a manservant implied that his artistic endeavors did not exactly keep him in poverty. For some reason, Julia had not expected this home.

Michael kissed her fervently. Julia slightly protested that his servant could see it. Michael did not care in the least.

"Jonathan is my cook, my housekeeper, my father-confessor and, at times I even believe he thinks that he's my mother." Michael laughed, and his fervent lips again pressed firmly against Julia's mouth, his strong arms encircling her.

"Listen, my darling Madcap," he said, "we are here in an artist's home and not at a public exhibition. You can be *too* careful, you know."

"That's all well and good," Julia replied, "but I intend to keep my reputation blameless as far as the members of my own society are concerned. Why don't you give me the address of your tailor, and I will ask him to make me some men's clothes."

"A splendid idea! Then we can be really good friends. We can travel wherever we want, go hiking, out for picnics, and the only thing

146

people will think is that I am a queer! But for you, my darling, I would do anything. I have an even better idea. After breakfast I shall send Jonathan to my tailor and have the man come here. In that case he will never be able to find out who you are!"

Jonathan entered and announced that breakfast was ready. They walked into a small, cozy dining room. A table for two had been set.

"Oysters, truffles, and champagne," Julia exclaimed, adding laughingly, "are you planning a two man orgy?"

"As I said, my darling, with you and for you I'll do anything."

"That sounds dangerously like a proposal."

"And what of it. I want to spread the whole world before your feet. My whole world! See here . . . the bedroom, the kitchen, the living room, my workroom, the dining room, and a splendid little garden. Dearest lady, I want you to consider it your home."

They had breakfast. Jonathan served, but he appeared only when Michael rang for him. Michael was overjoyed to discover that this fascinating woman understood him immediately, regardless of the subject. He seriously thought about making her his life's companion. This was the first time he had found a beautiful woman who understood the meanderings of his artistic mind.

Jonathan served coffee and cigarettes, not in the least surprised that Michael asked him to put it on a little end table next to the couch.

"Thanks, old man," Michael said when Jonathan announced that he would be on his way to the tailor, "and don't forget to tell my model

—you know, the little brunette—that she does not have to come in today."

Though nothing in the world was more natural than that an artist would have a model, Julia could not help but feel a little pang of jealousy. A cloud crossed her lovely face.

"What's wrong, my little Madcap?" he asked. "Why do you all of a sudden look so stern and reserved?"

Without thinking about the implications of her question, Julia asked, "What model?"

As Michael was too much a man of the world not to understand what was in Julia's mind, he was also smart enough not to show it.

"Oh, her," he said. "She is a little girl of about fourteen years I would guess. I saw her yesterday walking around in Montmartre and asked her to come in and pose for some sketches. I am planning to do a painting of a little gypsy beggar, and I think that she is just about perfect for it. If you want to, I'll show you some of the preliminaries I did of her from memory."

Julia had regained her confidence again and Michael, noticing this, put his arms around her shoulder and pulled her toward him. A warm feeling flowed through Julia. She had not known this since the day Count Saski had left her to marry the choice of his Aunt Athena. It seemed ages ago now. She relaxed against Michael's strong shoulder with a contented sigh.

"Madcap . . . you are so beautiful," the young man whispered.

Madcap did not answer, but Michael's hand upon her heart could feel it pound strongly.

"You know, darling, that the sight of beauty is headier than the best wine to an artist. Can't

148

you feel how my entire heart cries out for you? Can you understand that this moment will decide whether my life is going to be happy or unhapy? I beg of you, be a woman, a real woman, and don't play with me. Please, don't let convention force you to hide your true feelings. Tell me, do you love me as much as I love you?"

Julia did not answer. Her head nestled more comfortably against his shoulders. She looked up at him, and their lips met in a passionate kiss. When they broke loose to take a deep breath, they both knew that they were in love with each other. Past and present disappeared. Time stood still, and they were both drunk with heavy passion. Michael stammered, "I love you . . . please, be mine . . . always," and his hands fumbled around with her clothing. He began to get impatient and finally ripped the buttons of her pearl-gray travel costume.

A cloud of delicious perfume came toward him. It was a mixture of pure woman smell and costly essence. It fired his passions to greater action and he simply riped off the remaining clothes. He caressed her white shoulders with passionate kisses. It was not the brutality of rape, but the tender caress of a connoisseur.

During this wild embrace his hands worked quickly, unbuttoning Julia's bodice, stripping her stockings, her corset, and finally the last part of her clothing fell to the floor and she lay naked in his arms.

She had made one last defensive gesture; one could not call it a struggle, and he knew that it was the last vestige of convention which still had a strong hold on her. But he also knew

149

that he was winning. She was sighing happily under his expert caresses. He became bolder. He tickled the thighs of the beautiful young woman with his blond beard.

Julia was stretched halfway across the couch now, and only the goose pimples on her tender skin were silent witnesses of the intensity with which she received Michael's love. The artist pushed her softly back upon the pillows, threw her legs around his neck and opened his trousers which suddenly had become quite uncomfortable because of the enormous bulge.

The firm, round thighs were now directly in front of him, their apex crowned by her lovely Venus mound covered with radiant black curls. It drove him out of his mind. His lips eagerly sought the costly treasure, but Julia had had enough foreplay—she wanted the real thing. There are people who are that lucky! Once they meet the right person, an elaborate necking and petting is not necessary. They keep that as a dessert rather than using their energy for the hors d'oeuvre. Both Michael and Julia belonged to these elect people; their ecstasies lasted for hours and hours.

They did not dream about separating their bodies after they had been shaken by the paroxysms of their lovemaking. Instead, they kept arms and legs intertwined, their lips warmly together, whispering endearing words to one another, especially, "I love you."

And then, after only a few minutes, they would go at it again with as much enthusiasm as if they had been love-starved for weeks.

CHAPTER TEN

The hours had flown by, and it was almost four o'clock in the afternoon. Julia de Corriero and Michael Lompret were still closely pressed together. Michael was slowly rubbing Julia's backside and rump, and the effect was magical. She pressed herself closer against him and her breathing quickened. He kept it up for quite some time and finally she was slowly spasming again.

"And now, my darling, pull up your legs, brace yourself, and lift up a little bit . . ."

Michael had been fully in command all day, though there was really no need for him to tell her what to do. She had lifted herself so high that he had to watch out not to lose his equilibrium.

"Ooh . . . I can't . . . any longer."

"Am I . . . tormenting you, dearest Madcap?"

"You must . . . be . . . kidding! Oooooh . . . aah!"

Her passion was burning wildly again.

"I . . . can't . . . can't . . . stand . . . it . . ."

Her breathing was slow and heavy; she kept hovering on the verge.

"Oooooooh! Now!"

It wouldn't come.

Michael doubled his thrusts and soon his rod overflowed. She started to quiver under him, closed her eyes and her little pleasure fountain started to bubble. It filled to the brim and flowed over. They both fell in a voluptuous swoon and remained, bone tired, belly to belly.

Michael looked down upon her passionate

151

cunt. The black curls were covered with light foam, the rose-colored lips peeked through and smiled at him. Julia pulled him back on top of her, kissing him passionately. Finally, after all those many, many hours, they feel asleep, holding each other in a firm embrace.

But all good things have to come to an end, and this time it came in the form of old Jonathan. He had come back from his mission, and, knocking at the door of the studio, he had received no answer. He bent down to peek through the keyhole, murmuring, "Dammit, it must be great to be young and beautiful like those two there. Oh, well, I have had my time. Too bad it was so long ago."

He shuffled to the kitchen to fix tea and food, knowing what Michael would want around five o'clock.

And that's what happened. At precisely that time the couple was awakened by the ringing of the doorbell.

"It seems that Jonathan isn't back, yet," Michael yawned. "I wonder who that could be?" And as he walked over to the window to peek through the curtains. He saw his tailor.

Jonathan meanwhile had opened the front door, telling the man that his Master was very busy in his studio and would he, the tailor, please make himself comfortable in the waiting room.

"It's the tailor, darling," Michael said. "Do you still want to visit me in men's clothing?"

"Heavens no," Julia said, throwing her arms around his neck. "I have come here as a woman, I have been treated as a woman, and I am very, very glad that I am a woman. I would die of shame if I had to sneak into your home dressed as a man."

"I, too, don't think that I would really like the switch. It seemed the only way out this morning, but I am afraid that you would lose something in the transformation."

"Why don't you send him away."

"Go into my bedroom, and I will call Jonathan." Julia quickly picked up her clothing and went into Michael's bedroom.

"Jonathan, I am sorry, but please send the tailor away. It was all a mistake. Tell him that he will have to come back next week, and that I need a travel costume. But today I unfortunately cannot give him any of my time."

Jonathan grumbled something which Michael could not quite understand and then he said, more clearly, "I am sorry, Sir, but I could not find that model."

"Oh, she can go to hell," Michael said airily.

"To hell," the old servant thought when he went to tell the tailor about the new orders. "It seems that this latest love has really gotten to his heart. Well, let's face it, the sight of this beautiful woman makes me wish that I could not only get it up, but keep it there."

"And prepare us something to eat," Michael called after him.

"It will be ready when you are," Jonathan answered.

But Michael did not hear him. He was fascinated by his Madcap who was washing herself, douching and combing her beautiful, long black hair. Julia, of course, had no idea that she was being watched and leisurely finished her toilet. Michael was so riled up that he would have pushed open the door, taken her in

153

his arms and started all over again, were it not for the fact that Jonathan would soon be back in the studio with tea and food.

A few minutes later, Julia entered the studio, immaculately dressed and made up. She smiled at him and their hands found one another.

"And, my darling, did you find whatever you needed in my bachelor household," Michael smiled.

"Oh, yes, everything . . . and then some."

Michael blushed.

"I must tell you something," Julia continued. "My heart was dead when I entered your home this morning. And now that I am leaving it is alive again, full of hope and love."

"Do you have to leave?"

"Unfortunately, yes. But I can't wait till we see each other again."

"Darling, we have only known each other one week, but we have become one. I know that I belong to you, and that you belong to me. But all I know is that you are Madcap. Please, tell me your name."

"The world knows me as Donna José de Corriero, and some still remember me when I was the Viscountess Saniska. But for you, darling, I am Julia."

And at the same moment, all the plans which had been hatched for the house in the Rue Charles V were forgotten. Julia was in love, deeply in love, and she had decided to bare her heart to the man to whom she had already given her body to the fullest extent possible.

"Oh, Julia, you have made me happy with your confession. But why, my dear child, do

154

you have to leave? Stay with me for the night."

"No, I have given orders to be picked up at the station at ten o'clock, and my servants think that I went to see my sister who lives in the country. No, no! I have to be there on time."

"Fine, then let's see what Jonathan has cooked up for us."

Just at that moment Jonathan entered to announce that a repast had been served. He saw that Julia looked as immaculate as if she had just come out of the hands of her chambermaid. And his master talked to her as if she were a patron who had come to order some paintings.

"Oh, well," he thought when he left the studio, "these people of the world seem to enjoy faking it. If it gives them their jollies, who am I to say something about it. But, if I had not looked through the keyhole and seen for myself that they were screwing their hearts out, I would have never guessed."

Meanwhile Julia and Michael were doing honor to Jonathan's cookery.

"You said, darling," Michael began, "that your heart was dead when you entered this home. Would it be possible to tell me a little bit more about yourself. Don't you think that I deserve your trust? Surely you have loved and suffered, of that I am sure. And you could no longer believe that happiness was possible for you. Am I right?"

"You are close enough."

"Would you mind telling me the details?"

"Curiosity killed the cat."

"I don't want lurid details, but I feel a little possessive toward you, and I have great plans for the future. I would not want to start off with misunderstandings. Tell me about your husband: was he young or old, did you love him?"

"He was seventy-eight . . ."

"Seventy-eight," Michael exploded, and an icy hand gripped around his heart. This beautiful creature had given herself to a senile old man in exchange for money and a title? Maybe the old man had been very poor . . . desperately Michael tried to create a thousand excuses, but the word seventy-eight stuck in his throat like the bone of a fish.

Julia noticed his consternation and she continued. "He died two years ago, and I will honor his memory forever, because he was a dear and fatherly friend, as good a friend as any girl could wish for."

"A father? A friend?" Michael asked.

"Yes! A father," Julia emphasized.

"Nothing more?"

"No, nothing more."

But suddenly Julia understood. She could read Michael's mind as if it were an open book, and her eyes blazed.

"Do you think . . . oh! This thought is disgusting and insulting!"

"Why, darling?"

"Because you think that I belonged to him, and shared his bed!"

"Well, till now I have always believed that a man takes himself a wife so that he can go to bed with her."

"It so happened that this was not the case of Don José de Corriero, and if you care to listen, you doubting Thomas, I shall tell you about my life."

"Oh, a general confession."

156

"If you want to call it that."

"Well, my dear penitent, I promise complete absolution beforehand." Michael's tone was light and airy, because he did not want a repeat of Julia's sudden temper flare-up. "Sit down next to me, my daughter, and explain to me how it was that you had a husband who was only a father and friend but, still, managed to lack that which distinguishes an innocent virgin from an experienced woman."

"I'll confess, dear Father." Julia fell into the game. She lowered herself and sat between his thighs, her head resting in his lap.

"Now I understand why so many father confessors get into trouble," Michael jokingly said, to make it easier for Julia to begin. "And, my dear Madcap Julia, I promise you that I will reward your confession with one of mine."

She told him about her early life with Aunt Briquart who had raised her and her sister, Florentine as if they were her own children while in reality their father, Hector, was only a distant cousin. How her sister, Florentine had married the only relative of the Colonel, Aunt Briquart's late husband, and how she, shuddering at the thought of becoming an old, rich man's wife, had given herself to the young and dashing Count Saski. How she had become his mistress, and how his Aunt Athena who in faraway Poland held the purse strings had forced him to marry Lady Wilhelmina Soustbacka. Then she told him about the fatherly help she had had from General Don José de Corriero and how she and the old man had taken care of Don José's dearly beloved mistress, the Baroness de Sambreval. She talked about her sorrows, her dashed hopes, and about the great help of Don José's unwavering friendship. How, when death neared, he had wanted to make her his heir, and had done so by asking her hand in marriage. She talked about everything, except one. She never mentioned her wild night with the Count de Paliseul. It certainly had slipped her mind.

"And what have you been doing these past two years?"

"These past two years," was the evasive answer, "I have been waiting for my heart to heal, and for the confirmation that I was still desirable and capable of making love. And all three have happened today. I could sing Halleluja! And that, dear Father Michael, is my confession. If I have forgotten a few details, they will undoubtedly pop up during our future conversations."

"No, my dearest child, on the contrary. We shall definitely forget them. Close the pages of that book, and start out on a new life."

"Do I have to say, 'mea culpa, mea culpa, mea maxima culpa'?"

"No, my precious, because you are blameless. You have loved, and you have believed. If you had had any doubts, you would not have been in love. Go in peace. I not only absolve your heart from all sin, but my love and respect for you have enormously grown. You are the woman of my dreams, and I know that together we shall be very happy. Go in peace, my child!"

"And now, dear sir," Julia said, getting up from her knees, "it is your turn."

Michael had nothing of importance to confess. He had fallen in and out of love with more mistresses than he could remember, al-

158

ways searching for that feeling which now held him in its grip. He told about his youth, his young manhood, his desire to become an artist, and his father's—General Lompret's—disappointment that he did not wish to follow a military career.

At ten o'clock they were at the North Railway station in Paris, and Michael did not leave till he saw the equipage draw up in front of the station to pick up Julia. He watched the carriage disappear in the distance, and went home. At two the next morning he finally fell asleep.

CHAPTER ELEVEN

"And when will we see each other again," he had asked, just before Julia went toward the carriage.

"At my home, when I receive guests."

"Fine! But that is not enough!"

"Of course not. If you would like to come to the little chapel of St. John in Montmorency Forest, I will be there at ten in the morning."

"And what if it rains?"

"Then you can expect me to knock at your door."

When the day drew near, Michael prayed for the worst weather Paris had ever known. He wished it to rain cats and dogs, but unfortunately the sky was cloudless, the sun brilliant, and the breeze warm.

"Stupid sun," the young man exclaimed, "have you no heart at all?"

But at ten o'clock he was near the chapel, and his heart quickened when he saw Julia. She was happy about the beautiful weather, and enchanted that her newfound friend had come all the way to stroll with her through the woods.

Even though Michael would have infinitely preferred to have Julia in his home behind locked doors, he enjoyed the idea of a stroll in the woods and a picnic later.

Unfortunately, the young man had not counted on the wiles of mother nature. Normally, Michael was rather shy and chaste. He would only then fall in raptures when the woman inflamed his artistic nature first. It had very seldom happened that he went out to look for a woman simply to get rid of a physical need. Now that he was in love, it was impossible to control himself. He noticed the effect first when he kissed the hand Julia held out for him.

"For God's sake, Julia, don't look at me that way."

"Why?"

"I am about to commit a crime."

"What?"

"Please, don't ask me!"

"You scare me. I want to know. What crime?"

"Despite all these people walking here, despite the policemen who are riding around on their horses, I am going to rape you in the first clearing I see!"

"What gets you so excited all of a sudden?"

"All of a sudden? Darling, all I really want to do is hop in bed with you. I cursed this beautiful weather this morning, because I had hoped to hold you in my arms all day and night. But you can trust me, darling. No matter how much I want to throw you down in the first clearing, I shall contain myself. I do not wish to ruin something which is so beautiful—namely, our relationship.

"But please, please, darling," he pleaded, "come home with me to Paris tonight."

"Your home?"

"Yes!"

"And what would the venerable Jonathan say to that?"

"Him? I would tell him to keep his mouth shut!"

"And if anybody would see me enter at such a late hour. What would people think?"

"If you care about that, my darling, I will tell them that I am painting your portrait. I won't tell them that like the labors of Penelope, I shall never finish it. Please, Julia, you do love me, don't you?"

"Of course, my big boy. And to prove it to you, I am going to do something terribly silly."

"Now you are making sense."

"But, dearest Michael, you must give me your solemn promise that you not remember tomorrow what is going to happen tonight!"

"I promise anything, darling. What is your plan?"

"You go back to Paris, as you planned. But be in front of St. Paul's church at nine o'clock."

"The one in the Marais district?"

"Yes."

"And then?"

"You'll see . . . or are you afraid?"

"I am only afraid never to see you again."

"I swear to you that I will pick you up."

"Then I will go now and practice patience."

*   *   *

Nine o'clock. The sonorous bells rang out the time, and Michael was standing on the steps of the church, his heart pounding. At the same time a simple cab halted, and a heavily veiled woman came out, walking toward him. He ran toward her, grabbed her hands.

"Well, is this punctual enough?"

"I thought it would never become nine!"

"Come," she said, taking his arm. She led him through a series of dark and dank little streets.

"Where on earth are you taking me in this God forsaken neighborhood?"

162

"Why there," and Julia took a little key from her pocket, opening a heavy gate.

They were in a huge garden.

"Wow! You seem to know your way around here!"

"Possible."

They crossed the garden and soon, as the reader undoubtedly has guessed, they were at the foot of the huge stairs which led to the mansion on the Rue Charles V. The lanterns were burning but there was no servant in sight.

"It seems to me as if we are in a magic palace," Michael finally said.

"Yes, we are in the palace of love."

"That's right, because we are here."

Suddenly, as if she had come out of the ground, Dorothy stood in front of her mistress. "Oh, it's you, Madame," she exclaimed in surprise.

"Yes, and what is so surprising about that? I did not expect you to be here. Why are you?"

"Madame Evergreen asked me. Do you want me to leave?"

"No. Light my room and help me dress."

Dorothy disappeared and a few minutes later Michael Lompret found himself in the boudoir of Madame Pomegranate Flower, being the first to see her without her mask.

He was too much of an artist not to notice the almost lascivious—though extremely tasteful—decoration of the place.

It would be untrue to state that he was happier here than in his own studio, which was simple compared to the sumptuous surroundings of the little palace on the Rue Charles V. Something had been added, though.

He no longer was confronted by a woman

who desired nothing but to be subdued. He found a female who gave herself freely, enthusiastically, who screamed at the peak of her highest lust, who squirmed, kissed and bit, who was well versed in every possible passionate position, whose body was feverish with lascivious desire and who knew precisely what to do to make a man drunk with lust and love.

Upon the big bear rug in front, and later upon the blankets of the enormous bed, Michael Lompret went through a battle of love such as he had never experienced in all his born days. Protected by heavy walls, secure in the knowledge that there would be no possible distraction, the refined comfort, and an enchanting, beautiful woman . . . who could possibly have said that Michael Lompret was not the happiest man in the world.

He was barely alone with his girl friend, had barely satisfied his curiosity glancing around the rooms they went through when Michael again felt the same desire which had so unexpectedly taken hold of his senses that morning in the forest. And, to be perfectly honest, Julia had similar desires.

Even though her memory of the night with the Count de Paliseul was not one of her happiest, the marvelous hours she had spent in Lompret's embraces had wiped it away. She had found in Michael's arms that physical ecstasy which once only Gaston Saski had given her. And, since Michael was stronger and younger, it was clear to her that it could only be better than ever. Especially since they knew each other already, there was no need for hesitant preparations, drawn out preliminaries and all the other niceties which had made her feel like a rutting courtesan and which, obviously, had been the thought of Raoul. Oh, could she ever forget that miserable rogue!

Dorothy helped her change quickly.

She looked charming and enticing, dressed only in a Chinese kimono made out of extremely thin, sheer silk which covered her light chemise. Her naked feet were kept warm by fur lined slippers. Michael swept her off the floor and held her in his strong arms. Then he sat down and held her on his lap. The entire atmosphere had made it abundantly clear to him that his woman was very experienced, and therefore he did not bridle his own unlimited imagination.

His hands wandered quickly across intimate paths, caressing the slender alabaster columns at whose top the love grotto awaited. He felt around in the thicket which covered it and did not hesitate to separate the finely curled pubic hairs to look at this beautiful, rosy slit. He feverishly took off his own clothes and showed himself to the young woman in the full glory of his young manhood. With an exclamation of joy, Julia threw herself on his chest and he lifted her high in his arms as if she were a little child. He held her behind up higher than her head, kissing the marvelous buttocks wildly. Then he put her down upon the bear rug, keeping her in the same position because he was going to penetrate her from behind. No sooner thought than done, and his expert fingers played around with her clitoris. She had a long, shuddering orgasm almost immediately —a double exclamation of joyful ecstasy, because Michael, too, could no longer hold in and his hot juices squirted with enormous strength deep into Julia. The two lovers rolled around upon the carpet. For a moment they thought they were going to die, but soon their pounding hearts subdued, and consciousness returned.

Michael was now wild with lust and desire. His nerves were taut, overstimulated; he had long been waiting for this exercise. He realized that this woman fully matched his own hot temperament and his attacks doubled and tripled in any possible way his wild imagination could think of. Their lips ground together, his hairy chest mangled Julia's ripe breasts and both thought they would die of sheer happiness.

Julia's eyes ranged over her lover's body. His broad, muscular shoulders and arms, his curly haired, well defined chest, his flat belly and narrow waist, hard buttocks and long, muscular legs. His large, dangling testicles were half lost in the shaggy covering of blond hair. She began to stroke them and soon his rod jutted out over her again, thick and straining.

Michael quickly lay down against her once more, running his hands in fluid movements over her body so that she began to quiver and tremble. He caught her hand, pulled it against his penis and she closed her fingers around the stiff, bursting flesh. Michael's whole body was alive; he had to do it again.

Picking her up from the floor, he threw her upon the huge bed. He moved one leg over Julia, lowering it between hers, and moving his body onto hers he drew over his other leg in the same movement so that his hips were between Julia's thighs. He drove into her again.

His body again was one great yearning, a

hot, jellied feeling concentrated in his loins.
He began to grunt, his breath grating in his
throat. He held Julia with all his force, crushing her, rendering her body helpless. He
reached down, drawing her legs apart and up
around him, plunging deeper into her love nest.
There was nothing gentle about the union.

Julia's hips wriggled and swayed under him,
crinkling the flesh of her belly in little ridges.
Her thighs held him clasped as if she wanted
to hold him there forever. Her moans became
the deeper, fuller moans of accepted challenge.
Her eyes were closed as her fingers stroked
down over his cheeks and drew his face onto
hers for his mouth to make an outlet for her
searching, moving tongue.

With quick, furious movements of his hips,
Michael thrust into her, pulled out all the way
and thrust into her again, regulating his speed
to make sure that Julia would be fully satisfied.
His prick seemed to be burning as if it were
on fire. Amazingly, Julia's channel was still as
tight and tender as that of a virgin. It grasped
him as if it were a tight fitting, warm glove.
He was always pushing against a slight force
which agonizingly forced back his skin, contracting around his knob in exquisite agony.

Suddenly Julia's whimpering became a more
prolonged and consistent moaning. She grabbed
at his thighs where they pressed at the under-
sides of hers, pulling them furiously against
her. Her whole tender frame began to writhe
and twist in agony, and in the rushes of air
which burst from her throat, Michael sensed,
rather than heard, whispered pleadings for
more speed.

Her tiny hands clutched him with the force

of a madman, digging into his shoulders. Her knees stretched back, her buttocks wriggled under his strong thighs, her face contorted and then her whole body was wracked and tormented in a series of unending convulsions. Her soft passage reached the extreme of sensation and the liquid juices exploded as the breath was drawn from her body in a furious aching sign. Michael had won!

As he felt the channel grow big around his penis, he forced himself deeper into Julia, holding her firmly, pressing and grinding against her without jerking his hips. His head swayed in ecstasy and then he withdrew, thrust slowly in again—and again—and with a last deep surge, his love juices broke through, spattering in swift spurts high up in Julia's body. He rammed into her, gasping, until the very last of his emotion had been drained from him. He settled slowly down on her hot, soft body and lay, crushing her breasts and belly with his weight until they both fell asleep from complete exhaustion.

When they woke up in the morning next to each other in the wide bed, they barely looked human.

A cold bath and a heavy breakfast with lots of coffee revived them quickly. Nevertheless it took several days before they had completely recuperated from that night. It had one advantage; Michael could set up the painting he was going to make of Julia without any interruptions other than a kiss, or a meal taken together. During those sessions heart and mind won out over pure lust and passion, thus weaving their lives together in such a way that only catastrophe could have separated them.

168

Dorothy did not particularly like the new friend and Julia had a lot of explaining to do. It was very important for her that Dorothy would like Michael, because Julia had decided to take her lover to La Bidouze castle, and she would have suffered if the separation would have had to be a painful one.

La Bidouze was a beautiful castle on the banks of the river by the same name in the Pyrenees. It belonged to the General's inheritance, and Julia had long ago decided to restore the old building and to live there several months out of the year. And nothing was more obvious to explain than the presence of a painter.

As always, Dorothy undertook all the preparations, and she was slightly mollified by the idea that she was still indispensable to her mistress. She had been terribly miffed because Julia had not used her sphinx intrigue to come up with the one and only. She consoled herself however, by poo-poohing this affair with the thought that it was only a passing phase.

Before he left, Michael asked, "Darling, where are we?"

"At my home."

"Your home? I thought you live on the boulevard St. Michel?"

"Officially, yes. This is my Buen Retiro, my little love nest."

"Little!! Is this the place where this Polish Count of yours . . ."

"Michael, dear . . . your jealousy is showing. No, it is not!"

"How do you explain that this whole place is designed to receive a lover?"

Julia knew that Michael would form his

own opinions unless she told him the truth. She spared him a few lurid details—and also forgot to mention the Count de Paliseul—but she did tell about the terrible loneliness that she and her sister had felt after both had become widows at such a young age. She told him about her incestuous affair with her sister, and how Dorothy, her trusted chambermaid, had joined in the lovemaking. Then she told him about Dorothy's plan to buy this home, and the intrigue with the sphinx.

"You are two terribly perverted sisters."

"I think, my dear, that in the past few days you have gathered enough proof that you are wrong. At least, as far as I am concerned. I prefer the real thing infinitely above all these artificial means."

"You are right. I was only kidding, because I see absolutely no crime in a method of preference. It's about the same with people who prefere Champagne over Burgundy. Both are very heady, but the taste is different. But I am glad you have told me, and I promise that you can count on my complete discretion."

"I don't doubt that for a minute, Mister Lompret, and I would call it an honor, if you, kind Sir, would show up at my next reception. I will be glad to serve you personally."

"And I, dear Lady, am equally as honored to accept your kind invitation."

* * *

No one was more curious that afternoon of Donna de Corriero's reception than her sister, Florentine Vaudrez. She almost burst with curiosity, nearly jumping up from her seat

170

when the servant announced Sir Michael Lompret.

She saw a man of the world, extremely good looking, who greeted the lady of the house with mannered, formal politeness. Even Florentine, who knew all the details of their love bouts, would never have guessed that Michael Lompret and her sister knew each other intimately.

After he had left, the two sisters looked at each other.

"A well brought up young man, your Michelangelo," Florentine said, slightly spiteful, adding hastily as Julia's eyes flared up, "Who knows? Maybe fate works better than our hideout on the Rue Charles V."

"I think it does, though our love nest is a brilliant invention."

"Isn't it, ladies?" Dorothy was eager for praise. "Neither one of you has been bored since we started this." And she emphasized the word "we."

"You are positively right, my dearest girl," Julia said, glad that Dorothy did not seem to be angered, "and since you have helped your fatherland above and beyond the call of duty, I bequeath to you the complete wardrobe of Madame Pomegranate Flower who, just last week, had to return to her social duties in faraway Andalusia."

CHAPTER TWELVE

"Next week, my dear big bad wolf, I am going to the Pyrenees," Julia de Corriero said one morning when she awoke in Michael's arms.

"You are going away? You mean we are not going to see each other again?"

"Who said anything about not seeing each other? Aren't you as free as I am? Who is there to prevent you from following me in a couple of weeks? I have an old castle down there which needs restoring. It is positively loaded with old paintings, and what is more natural than that you supervise the restoration? Besides, I am getting a little tired from the busy life in Paris, I want to leave my sister alone in our love nest and moreover, the castle is so far-away from the hustle and bustle of society that nobody, I am sure, will pay us a visit."

"Well, in that case, darling, I am not going to wait fourteen days. I'll follow you within a few."

"Fine, that's a date," she said as she opened her thighs to allow Michael Lompret full entrance with his big, throbbing prick.

* * *

Meanwhile, in Florentine's part of the building, near disaster struck. She was cavorting with Maxim de Berny, who was mumbling words of endearment to his Lady Evergreen whenever his mouth was not busy searching for her little clitoris.

He had just aroused a tremendous orgasm in his paramour and was coming up for air,

when Evergreen's mask slipped and, utterly flabbergasted, Maxim recognized her.

"My dearest Lady . . . you . . . you . . ."

"Oh, my God! Yes, it's me! That stupid
mask was smothering me. I do hope that you
will not use your knowledge to compromise me."

"Me? Compromise you! What do you take
me for? But let me tell you that women sure
have a knack for making things complicated. I
have longed for you ever since that night . . ."
here he stopped, because he did not want to
bring up certain things which Florentine might
want to forget.

"It would have been so much easier to pro-
tect you without all these sphinx secrets," he
continued.

"What do you mean?"

"Isn't that easy to understand?"

"No, not unless you explain yourself."

"Don't you understand? The members of
the Club de Topinambours have taken it upon
themselves to find out who these two mystery
women are. After all, both de Paliseul and I
have told them about our first adventure. Since
then, I have denied knowing anything more. I
did not want to give up my love because of the
curiosity of some members of my club. And,
let me tell you, my dearest, these members are
like bloodhounds, sniffing throughout Paris to
pick up the trail. Why didn't the two of you
trust the honor of two gentlemen?"

"In the first place, it was so amusing . . ."

"And in the second place?"

"What if we had not been so compatible?"

"I see, you mean if we had been like de Paliseul and Pomegranate?"

Florentine answered by nodding her head.

"And if I may ask, who is this dark Andalusian woman?"

"Her secrets are not mine. I do not have the right to tell you."

"Well, darling, you are right as far as that is concerned. But, now that I know your identity, the big problem remains—how to lead our bloodhounds on a wrong trail."

"How do you want to do that."

"Let me think about something." Maxim gave her a reassuring kiss, his hands lingering upon her beautiful golden fleece.

"In whose name is this house," he asked after several minutes.

"Felicitas'."

"The Negro woman?"

"Yes."

"And this precious woman is as much a Negro as I am, I dare presume?"

"You are right. But she is a very, very trustworthy servant."

"That I have noticed. In whose service is she?"

"Pomegranate Flower's."

"I think I have a good idea. Why don't we send de Paliseul an invitation from the Sphinx. He will be overjoyed to hear from his Pomegranate Flower, and undoubtedly tell everyone in the club about his new invitation. Then I will suggest to use this opportunity to uncover the secret of the two beautiful women. And you, my dearest, will have to make some arrangements with Felicitas, in whose name this house is registered, to give our friend de Paliseul a fitting reception."

"That sounds very exciting!"

"Fine! Then we will create a complication our friend shall never forget!"

"What a great idea!"

"But you must promise to help me!"

"Of course!"

"Great! Let's start the comedy tomorrow."

They went into several details, not forgetting that they had gotten together to make love. When Maxim left, he had given his Lady Evergreen more than ample proof that her trust in him had not diminished his love for her. Ten minutes after he had gone, Florentine was still recuperating from her last orgasm.

* * *

It was around four the next afternoon when de Paliseul excitedly waved his invitation before the members of the club. He was overjoyed.

"What are you waving there," Maxim asked him.

"That Pomegranate Flower has finally changed her mind," de Paliseul exclaimed.

"Bah! Pooh! Bullshit," were just a few of the words that could be heard from the membership.

"See? It's the sign of the sphinx," said de Paliseul, furious that his fellow members did not believe him.

"Do you remember your promise, de Paliseul?" Maxim asked innocently.

"I sure do, and I aim to keep it!"

"And we shall be very happy, once and for all, to lift the veil of secrecy which hides the ladies Evergreen and Pomegranate Flower!"

"But I don't know how to do it!"

"Very simple," Maxim said hypocritically.

"We rent another coach which looks like any normal cab, but instead of an old nag, we make sure that it has a very spirited horse. All you have to do is to tell us when and where."

"Nine o'clock sharp, the tenth street lantern on the Champs Elysées."

At precisely the indicated time, the black equipage with the sphinx emblem stopped in front of the lantern under which de Paliseul was waiting. The Negro woman showed her face, and, overjoyed with happiness, de Paliseul jumped inside. The coach rolled quickly away.

At a safe distance of about twenty paces however, it was followed by another coach which, as de Berny had suggested, looked for all the world like just another rent cab, but it had a spirited horse which easily could keep up with the carriage in front of it. Inside, bursting with tension and anticipation were the Counts de Berny, de Lyncent, and de Melreuse.

They turned into the Rue Charles V.

"So that's where they live?" the plotters said. "The next question is, how do we get in?"

The sphinx equipage stopped in front of the gate of an old building.

"Evergreen does not live here," de Berny said.

"Are you sure?"

"You don't think that I would brag about my visits to a dump like this? I make a bet that de Paliseul has given us one of his famous fantasy stories."

"That would be the limit!"

"I know that," de Berny exclaimed as if he suddenly got a brilliant idea, "let's surprise him!"

"How?"

176

"It should not be difficult to bribe the gate-keeper of such a cheap establishment."

They rang the bell, and the gate opened at a narrow slit. An old gatekeeper showed his face.

"We must," de Berny said, "speak to the gentleman who just came here to visit Madame Pomegranate Flower. It is very urgent that we see him at once. I hope you understand." And he gave the old man a couple of gold pieces.

According to previous instructions the old man led the visitors up the stairs to the second floor, pointing wordlessly at a little waiting room. Nothing the gentlemen had seen so far looked remotely like the fantastic descriptions they had received. In fact, to them it looked as if they were being received in a second class whorehouse.

"It does not exactly fit the description," de Lyncent remarked.

"No," Maxim answered, "it's not in the least what I have seen in the little palace of Evergreen."

The gentlemen were beginning to get impatient because they had to wait quite a while. Finally the old man returned. He motioned for them to be silent, and led them through another door, where they suddenly found themselves in a huge bedroom. It looked exactly like the one de Paliseul had described in such glowing colors, except for the fact that it was very dimly lit.

The three friends groped carefully around in the darkness when they heard two sudden exclamations and saw two bodies moving upon the bed.

"Excuse us," de Melreuse said, "it seems

that we have been led into the wrong room by mistake."

Suddenly all the lights in the room went on and the three friends saw their comrade, de Paliseul, in the process of attacking a woman sexually. Her mask had fallen from her face and . . . it was the face of Felicitas!

De Paliseul jumped up as if he had been bitten by a viper.

"I would have liked it much better, you dirty cocksucker," Felicitas screamed as if she were a real cheap whore, "if you could have kept your damned mouth shut. Are those guys gonna watch us fuck, or what? Why didn't you keep our secret? Please, come back here . . . you're the only one who can make me come!"

And with exaggerated tenderness, Felicitas threw her arms around the embarrassed de Paliseul's neck. He pushed her back.

"What do you mean pushing me, you bum! And what are those guys doing here anyway! I only fuck you for free . . . they can stand in line and pay like all the rest."

"You . . . you . . . are . . . the . . . Negro maid of P—P—omegra . . ." de Paliseul stuttered helplessly.

"What do you mean by 'Negro maid'? Do I look black?" And Felicitas, now standing on the bed, turned around and lifted her skirts, showing a huge pair of snowy-white buns.

"And this," she screamed in simulated anger, baring her voluptuous bosom, "are these tits you have been sucking black?"

The onlookers had to admit that this delicious pair of breasts was as white as the arse they had just viewed. They practically rolled on the floor, roaring with laughter.

"I don't know what you want, gentlemen," Felicitas said, "but you are in my house and I advise you to scram before I call the police. And you, you bastard," she turned to de Paliseul, "pick up your pants and don't let me ever see your face again. It's out . . . you hear . . . out! No more free screwing for you."

De Paliseul scrambled hastily into his clothes, and Felicitas threw a robe over her disarrayed clothes. She rang a bell, and the old man showed up again.

"You're fired, you miserable old scum," Felicitas screamed, throwing a half-crown at the old man, which he picked up hastily. "Your last job is to throw out these fine friends . . . if you can use that word!"

The old man led them crisscross through a series of dark corridors and hallways, down the stairs, and finally the members of the club found themselves in a little dark alley behind the Rue Charles V.

"So that was your gorgeous houri!" Again the friends broke out in a salvo of laughter. "We knew that you had a terrific imagination, de Paliseul, but to make a magical palace out of that dump, and a gorgeous creature out of a common whore takes quite a lot!"

"Gentlemen, gentlemen," de Berny said, trying to calm down the storm, "let's admit that she had a pair of beautiful breasts, and her buttocks weren't bad, either. I must admit that her language was not very ladylike, but one can't have everything for free."

"I think I'm going out of my mind," de Paliseul cried.

"I don't think so, my friend. After all, it is impossible to describe a face which was hid-

179

den behind a mask. Besides, every good doctor for the insane can tell you that the excitement and the intrigue will put things in your mind that are as real for you as if they had truly happened."

This was not exactly the consolation de Paliseul needed at the moment.

"Poor Paliseul, you've been tricked. Your imagination has ascribed qualities to a rather overaged courtesan, or possibly some rich old woman who couldn't possibly snare anyone without resorting to a bagful of tricks."

"And then," number three added, "the possibility does exist that you were the only man capable of satisfying an old whore."

The three broke out in tremendous laughter again.

"I've gone crazy . . . I must have gone crazy!" de Paliseul hailed a cab, and before his three club fellows could say anything else, the carriage drove away.

A few days later, in a duel, one of his friends wound up with a piece of lead in his shoulder, all honors were settled, and the routine in the Club de Topinambours was as of old.

It seemed that the entire episode had been forgotten. But it only seemed that way, because a terrible thirst for revenge had taken root in de Paliseul's heart, and he swore an oath that those who had made such a fool out of him would have to pay dearly for their fun.

*   *   *

Meanwhile, Maxim de Berny had seen to it that his two friends also took a cab to their homes and, when he was sure that nobody followed him, returned to the home in the Rue

Charles V, where he found Evergreen and Dorothy still in a hilarious mood.

"Well, what did you think of Dorothy's acting?" Florentine asked.

"It was marvelous, Dorothy! What an act! Oh, dearest Evergreen, if you could only have seen how she greeted us! You have a marvelous behind, Dorothy."

"Your Lordship is joking."

"Not at all, Dorothy, and as proof for my admiration, here are ten gold pieces."

"Your Lordship is too good. For this amount I am entirely at your service."

"I thank you, dear girl, but I wouldn't want to abuse your hospitality."

"And what did my lover have to say?" Dorothy was curious, not able any longer to wait for a detailed description.

The ladies got what they asked for and, when Maxim had finished they practically rolled on the floor with laughter. Especially when they heard that de Paliseul seriously thought about consulting a doctor for the insane.

Do we have to say that this pleasant evening ended with Maxim's eager lips between Florentine's shuddering thighs?

CHAPTER THIRTEEN

Archaeologists insist that the castle of La Bidouze was built in the early twelfth century.

It is nestled halfway into the mountains and it rules the river and the valley beneath it. From a distance it gives the impression of an enormous eagle's nest.

The parents of Don José de Corriero had lived and loved here; their son was born and brought up in the old castle, and his bones were now resting in the chapel with those of his parents and forebears.

From the outside, the building looked stern and foreboding. Generations of owners seemed to have concentrated on the interior of the castle. It was loaded with antiques: furniture, tapestries, paintings, and the library contained books that would have caused much mouth watering among librarians.

Julia waited impatiently for the arrival of her lover, not only because her body cried out for him, but also because she wanted to create some order into the accumulation of generations of her late husband's forebears. She was therefore terribly disappointed when, instead of her beloved Michael, a letter arrived from him, informing her than an old aunt of his was on her deathbed. As tenderly as possible the young artist wrote that he loved the old lady dearly and, though he missed Julia terribly, he had to go to Nimes and see his aunt before she died. He begged her to understand and promised to join her in a couple of days.

Julia, who now had nothing else to do but

wait for her lover's arrival, undertook various short trips through her new domain.

Then, unexpectedly, the caretaker of the castle died in a hunting accident. He left his little eight-year-old daughter behind. The poor child's mother had died in childbirth, so Julia decided to take care of the girl.

She had already noticed that no one in particular took any notice of the child, and made up her mind that she would take the girl with her to Paris.

"I have no children of my own," she told Dorothy. "I am rich, and I owe it to the child to see that she gets a good education."

"Madame is right," Dorothy answered. "If nobody takes care of this little tomboy, she will come to no good."

Julia took care of the little girl as if she were her own mother. Of course, the memory of her own youth, and the excellent care she had received from Aunt Briquart, may also have played a role. The girl took to her immediately, and she followed Julia like a shadow.

One day, when they returned from one of their trips to the castle, they saw a little boy sitting along the side of the road. It seemed that the child was very ill. He could have been at the most only twelve years old.

Julia got out of the carriage, asking him what was the matter.

"I am hungry."

"Poor child," Julia said. "Claire, give the boy your breakfast, and then run inside to get Dorothy."

"What's your name?"

"Pedro."

"Are you Spanish?"

"I think so."

"Where are your parents?"

"Dead."

"And where do you live?"

"Nowhere."

"How did you get here?"

"They put me in an orphanage."

"And?"

"I didn't like it."

The boy sized up this beautiful lady and he obviously decided that he could give her a little bit more information.

"I ran across the border, and I've been begging ever since."

"All by yourself?"

"Yes, and now I'm sick."

Julia looked at the boy. He was good looking, well developed for his age, though he was rather skinny. But with proper care and feeding, he promised to become one of those beautiful types which have made the men and women of Andalusia famous all over Europe. Meanwhile Dorothy had arrived and in a few short words Julia told her what she had heard. The women decided to keep the boy at La Bidouze, at least till he had recuperated from his illness which Dorothy quickly diagnosed as plain starvation.

She also decided that the boy needed a good hot bath and plenty of scrubbing with lots of soap and water. When that was done they donned him Spanish clothing which looked very good on him. In a few days Pedro and little Claire were the best of friends.

"If Michael wants it," Julia said, "he can do the same for Pedro as I am doing for Claire, and maybe the two children can get married when they have reached the proper age."

And, since they could not make a decision for Pedro till Michael showed up, the boy stayed at the castle.

The days came and went, almost every one of them brought a passionate letter from Michael, but the story was basically the same. His dear aunt kept hovering between life and death; she did not want her beloved nephew to leave, and it seemed that patience was about the only thing Michael and Julia would be able to exercise.

Julia took her new mother role very seriously—she taught the child to read and write, and to have good manners. One can imagine her fury when, one day, she discovered her adopted daughter on her back in the grass, her little legs spread, allowing Pedro to examine her very carefully. His main interest was in his little companion's lower belly where his fingers were probing with an expertness one would not expect from a little boy barely twelve years old.

The children were so absorbed in their game that they did not notice the arrival of Julia and Dorothy. Julia put her fingers on her lips and with a few quick steps, she suddenly stood in front of the startled children. She yanked Claire by one arm, brushing the girl's skirts down, while Pedro tried to run away.

"Here, boy!" Dorothy jumped forward and grabbed him. "What are you two doing there! I'll sure ask Madame to punish you severely!"

"Pedro wanted it," the little girl cried.

"That does not mean you have to give it, young lady. And Dorothy is going to teach you that from now on you should not lightly follow a boy's desires."

Julia broke a few twigs from the nearest bush and handed them to her maid. "Lift the skirts of this foolish girl and give her a sound thrashing."

Dorothy grabbed the girl around the waist, pulled up her skirts and painted the little white behind with a few furious red strips. Claire screamed as if she was being slaughtered, her little legs trampled helplessly and she tried to no avail to wriggle out of Dorothy's strong grip.

"And now," Julia said, when Dorothy put the screaming child back on the ground, "I advise you never to be discovered in such a position again till you are quite a lot older."

Claire disappeared quickly.

Pedro still stood at the same spot. He had not moved a muscle.

"And you, young man, since you are older than the girl, and since you were the one who seduced her, will get a sounder thrashing than a weak woman can give you. I am going to call the gardener."

"What for?"

"To give you a sound thrashing."

"I kill him if he touches me."

"Is that so? We'll see about that."

"If I have to be punished," the boy said with a sigh, "it should be done by my father, and not by a servant."

"But you don't have a father."

"Then I'll wait till Mister Lompret arrives."

"That may be quite some time."

"I can wait."

"No nonsense, boy. I am going to call the only man present."

"I'll never allow that man to touch me. Honest! I'll run away. And since you took me in, you are more or less my mother. You are the only one who has the right to punish me."

Julia recognized the proud Spaniard in him, and it flashed through her mind that this orphaned boy might once have been from a good family.

"If that's your wish, young man," she said therefore, "so be it. But don't be deluded. If I set my mind to it, I can give you a solid thrashing."

"I deserved it," was the boy's only answer.

Julia did not exactly want to whip the boy out in the open, so she ordered him to go inside and wait for her in her boudoir.

The boy obeyed.

Julia locked the door behind her. Her boudoir was at the end of a long hallway, and no one would be able to hear the protestations she fully expected. She took off her hat, pulled up her sleeves, and Pedro, who till now had been very calm and almost in control of the situation, began to show signs of nervousness. He saw that she rolled the big armchair into the middle of the room and knew that Julia was dead serious. He understood that the critical moment had approached, and he fell on his knees, pleading for mercy in a loud voice.

But Julia's mind remained unchanged. After all, it would have been unfair to punish Claire, and to let Pedro get away with it.

"If you don't obey, I can always call the gardener," she threatened. The boy quieted down immediately.

"Come on, unbutton your pants."

187

And when Pedro did not obey quickly enough, Julia's expert fingers loosened his buttons and the boy's pants fell to the floor before he had had a chance to grab them and hold on to them. Then she pulled him across the arm of the chair with her left hand, lifted his shirt, and with her other hand she gave him twenty resounding slaps till his buttocks began to redden visibly. The boy howled as if Julia was about to murder him.

Madame de Corriero, exhausted by this work, which she was not used to at all, fell down upon the couch. She was astonished to see that Pedro, though crying, did not seem to think about putting his pants back on.

The boy, who was still sobbing, rubbed his sore behind, but remained motionless across the arm of the chair. Julia's surprise became even greater when she noticed something which she had least of all expected.

Either Pedro was far ahead of his age, or he had lied about it. His prick was standing up and had a size which would have made a traveling monk jealous.

"Well, well," Julia said to herself, "that's funny."

"Come on, dress yourself," she said in a loud, commandeering voice, "and don't let me ever catch you doing such a thing again. I do not wish to punish you, but I shall not hesitate if the necessity arises."

The little scene stayed in the back of her mind, and Julia became more than slightly curious about the boy.

And, only a week later, Pedro was again ordered into Julia's boudoir. He had stolen several items from the pantry and was caught red-handed by Dorothy. He denied everything.

Julia was furious this time. She did not mind that the boy had taken some food, but in all the years she had known Dorothy, she knew her maid to be honesty itself.

"If you know what's good for you," she said to the boy, "you will be in my boudoir at one o'clock sharp." This was the time when all the servants took their siesta.

Julia had steeled herself, and she was awaiting the penitent with the firm intention of giving him a sound thrashing.

"You have stolen, and you have lied," she said. "This is almost unforgivable, and you'd better be prepared for severe punishment. Get yourself in position."

The boy blushed, but he did not obey her.

"Didn't you hear what I said?"

"Yes, but I am ashamed."

"If you don't feel shame when committing a crime, you shouldn't have to feel it for the punishment."

Pedro, who had been called into the boudoir at very short notice, had had no time to think about any good excuses. He also wore not much more than a pair of shorts and a shirt. Julia had no trouble at all undressing the boy and he stood mother naked before her in no time at all. Julia took a hazel rod, which she had acquired for this occasion and ordered the boy again to bend over.

"Do you want to use *that* for punishing me?" he asked, his eyes blazing, pointing at the rod in Julia's hand.

"Yes."

"I don't want that."

189

"I could not care less what you want or don't want. Come on, bend over!"

"No! Please, hit me with your hands as hard as you desire, but don't treat me like a dog as the English do."

But Julia stood firm. She took the boy across her knees and the rod whistled sharply through the air, hitting the boy's buttocks and making a red stripe—and another one, and another one. Soon his wriggling buttocks were covered with red weals, and his young muscles twitched in pain. Finally, since Julia was getting tired, she put the rod in one of the drawers of her makeup chest.

When Julia turned around, the boy was on his knees, crying, big tears rolled down his cheeks. It would have been rather naive to ask why he was bawling.

"I hope you regret your mistakes, and I also hope that further punishments are no longer necessary. You better learn how to behave from now on."

"I don't want any more . . . I don't want any more . . ." the boy sobbed uncontrollably.

"I am glad to hear that you don't want to do any more stealing or lying," Julia said. She felt sorry for the sobbing child, and she patted his head. "You know now that any transgressions will be followed by the necessary punishment, and if you promise to behave, I promise not to punish you again."

"No, you don't understand . . . I don't want any more punishment with that . . . that . . . bundle of sticks! Paulina always hit me with her bare hands!"

"Who is Paulina?"

"My big, married sister."

"And then?"

"I don't know how to tell you."

"Try me."

"Hit me with your hand like you did the first time, and I will show you."

Julia, curious now, gave him a few light slaps on his behind.

Suddenly, little Pedro grabbed her hand, and held it against his member which was showing signs of hardening. Without any shame he made Julia caress it, and soon it was hard and swollen, jutting firmly forward. Amazing, the prick of a full grown man on this young boy! Julia was flabbergasted, but at the same time intrigued and amused. She allowed the boy, who had clasped her hand firmly in his, to jack off his big organ.

"I assume you like it that way," she said with a smile.

"Oh, yes, I do, I do!" Pedro's eyes sparkled. "And if you like it too, you can punish me as often as you want, even if I haven't done anything."

Julia appeared so intrigued with this new twist that Pedro soon became a little bolder. He quickly opened one of the ribbons of her negligée, managing to free one of her breasts.

"Will you keep your hands to yourself?" Julia exclaimed.

But Pedro, whose eyes were burning like coals, had bent his head toward her and was sucking firmly on her nipple. Despite herself, Julia shivered and the nipple hardened till she thought her straining breast would burst. The glow shot through her body and her fleece began to get moist.

"Who taught you this," she gasped.

"Paulina," the boy said. "I saw her husband do it to her, and she laughed and then she began to shake; she almost fainted, but she told him that she loved it more than anything else. He also did a couple of other things, which I did not understand. That's why I was trying to find out with Claire when you caught us in the grass."

"Yes, yes, and if Dorothy and I had not arrived in the nick of time, you would have done it to her."

"I don't know, but I would have done the other thing which I did with Paulina whenever Manuel was not home."

"And what was that?"

"Wait . . ." and Pedro fell on his knees.

"Don't move," he said. "It feels very good. You are going to scream, and you are going to turn white, and you may even faint. But you have nothing to worry about. I am here with you . . . just let me do it . . ."

He burrowed his head under her clothes and his hot tongue disappeared between Julia's curly fleece. He licked and sucked so expertly that, indeed, Julia let out a sharp cry of delight!

"You no good little rascal," she exclaimed, but not after she had reached a shuddering climax. The boy's head came from under her clothing, and he looked at her with a triumphant grin.

"I didn't lie to you, did I?" he asked. "This is what makes women happy!"

"That is very well possible you . . . you . . ." Julia panted. "But if you ever tell anyone about what has just happened, I'll have you punished daily by the gardener with the biggest stick you have ever seen!"

"From now on I will always be good and obedient.   But you must promise me that I can come here from time to time."

"To be punished by me?"

"And for the other thing," the boy said with a sly smile.

"We'll see!   But for now, put your clothes back on and go!"

CHAPTER FOURTEEN

A few months were to go by before Michael finally could join his beloved at the castle of La Bidouze. It was obvious that Julia planned to spend a lot of time with him, and the remainder would be given to Claire, because Julia did not want the little girl to be alone with Pedro. And as far as Pedro was concerned, though he needed punishment more than ever, he did not get any. The boy missed his regular sessions in Julia's boudoir, and tried everything he could think of to get the so hotly desired punishment. Julia, on the other hand, did not dare to leave punishments up to the gardener, as she had threatened, because she was afraid that the boy might take revenge and talk about their rather regular sessions.

Finally her dearly beloved was there. To all the other servants, Michael Lompret was the famous painter from Paris, who had been engaged to restore the interior of the castle. Only Dorothy, of course, knew the real situation.

In the farthest room of the castle, nights of love were celebrated which made the empty corridors echo with sighs and moans.

About two weeks after Michael's arrival at La Bidouze, the happiness was disturbed by an oath!

They had just fallen asleep after a particularly exhausting love bout, when Julia awakened.

"What is it, my dear?" Michael murmured.

"I don't know. I just can't sleep. There is something wrong."

"Haven't you had enough?"

"Oh, yes!"

"You want more?"

Julia smiled. Now that Michael was awake, too, the feeling of being spied upon disappeared. "Are you still capable?"

"I don't know, but I'm willing to try."

"Let me try something, I know you'll like it." She did not tell him that she had learned this trick from a little boy, but she took the tip of his cock between left thumb and forefinger. She began to draw on it, as one pulls at a cow's udder for milk, but with exquisite gentleness. Then she grasped him at the very root, drawing her fingers slowly up to the tip of his prick and let go with a flick of her wrist. In no time Michael's organ was bogging and jerking in the air. It had been completely reinvigorated.

"The operation was a complete success," Michael smiled.

"Yes, sir, I have to agree, and from this moment on, it is all up to you. The man of the house always does. Maybe you can discover a few of my special talents."

"Isn't it dangerous to give me so much free rein. You disturbed my happy sleep, and I may not be all sweetness and light?"

"Oh, I trust you." Julia smiled. "I don't think that you want to tie me up and beat me. Though, of course I won't say no to a little voluptuous spanking."

"How about going in from the other way?"

"Anyway you want it," she giggled, tickling his balls.

He stroked her surging titties. "For right now, before I lose this wonderful hard-on, I'd like to screw you on all fours."

"Perfect. There! Is this the right position?"

She had turned her back to him, then got on all fours, slowly bowing her head to the rumpled sheets till her body was almost flat against the bed. Her magnificent, milky bottom cheeks reared up and because of her straddled knees, were deliciously distended. The soft pink lips of her pussy peeped out, framed by the black curls of her pubic hairs. Above, recessed in the shadowy furrow which cleaved her now provocatively undulating buttocks, appeared the crinkly rosebud of her anus.

"Ooh, dear . . ." Michael sighed, "you make the decision terribly difficult."

He took his place behind her, reaching to cup her dangling, firm breasts, luxuriating in the feel of her warm flesh and the friction of her enticing bottom against his belly. Arching himself, Michael went forward till the knob of his throbbing organ was clamped between the moist, soft lips of Julia's yawning pussy.

"Ooooh . . . it's nice this way . . . yes . . ." Julia panted.

"Exactly. Besides, this way I can feel the little nippings and kisses your tight little slit is going to give my weapon." He drew out, playfully prodding the secretive little rosette of her asshole. Julia squirmed and glanced back, murmuring, "Do tell me, if you are going to do it to me that way. I have to prepare for that, darling. Put a little bit of saliva on your member and go into it with your finger first. That would help a good deal."

"Another time, my love. I think for now that I'll be satisfied with your sweet tight cunt, provided you wriggle that lovely backside about. There!"

He inserted himself again, and this time

with a violent shove of his loins, he was imbedded up to the hilt inside her. A stifled gasp of pleasure broke from the pillow in which Julia had burrowed her face. She contracted her buttocks, relaxed them, trying to synchronize her gyrations with his ins and outs. He could feel the moist, hot clinging of her flesh against his driving, turgid weapon. His thumbs rubbed her nipples till they were flint-hard peaks of pure erotic pleasure. Slowly and methodically he fucked her lovely, crouching naked beauty, glorying in the tightness of her narrow sheath as it absorbed his prick. She spread her thighs as far as she could, shoving back her bottom to meet his rhythmic attacks.

There was no thunder and lightning; no sheltering earthquake this time. Julia took her lover with wriggling hips and energetic thighs. Each time he sank into her up to the hilt he could feel the pulsations of her very womb. It took a long time to build up the tension in his loins, making it possible to probe her responsive, warm sheath. Finally, Julia fluted little cries, begging and urging him to drive her to the zenith of fulfillment. When he began to quicken his thrusts, he could feel her body churn and jerk as the orgasm exploded within her. It made him, too, come in an ecstatic release.

Suddenly, Michael felt a short, stabbing pain in his shoulder, and when he grabbed, a child's dagger fell to the floor. A shadow rushed through the room.

"Who is there?" he called.

Julia lit the lamp, and they searched the room. They found nothing.

To call the servants and have them search the castle would have compromised both Julia and Michael. It could not have been a burglar, Michael thought, because this dagger belonged to a child. Who could have done such a thing? He shrugged off the whole thing and from now on he made sure that the door was firmly bolted.

But Julia had recognized the little dagger she had once given to Pedro to complete the Spanish costume he always wore on Sundays. She made up her mind to talk about it to the boy.

"Where is that little dagger I gave you? Did you lose it?"

"No, I didn't. You have it."

"So it was you last night."

"Yes."

"And why did you do such a terrible thing? You must know that it was a terrible thing you did."

"I have spent the last couple of days under your bed, and I don't want that man to do those things to you."

"What man?"

"The painter! Michael Lompret. I don't want him to embrace you like that. You never let me do it that way!"

"That's all I needed! Listen here, young man, Michael Lompret wants to be to you like a father. He wants to take care of your upbringing and education, and if you want to throw away your future, you just try one of those tricks again!"

"I hate him!"

"And I advise you to behave!" Julia and the boy looked at each other, eyes blazing.

Pedro said nothing, but from that day on he followed Michael like a shadow, pulling pranks and making a nuisance of himself, whenever he found a chance.

Julia had told him, of course, how she had found Claire and Pedro, and that she had plans for the children. Michael had agreed to take Pedro under his wings. But, one day, after he had found big globs of lard in his boots, one of his paintings crisscrossed with a knife, and all his paints mixed together in one bucket, Michael decided that the time for firmness had finally come.

He calmly stepped down from his ladder, grabbed the boy by the scruff of his neck, pulled down the child's pants and, with the flat of his hand, painted Pedro's buttocks a deep purple. Then he carried the screaming, struggling boy to the front door, and dropped him unceremoniously in front of the smirking gardener. He closed the door and went back to his work.

The gardener asked him with a sneer if he liked being thrashed by Michael as much as he liked it from Madame? White with fury, the boy ran to his room. And, when they called him that evening for dinner, Pedro was gone.

"Good riddance," Michael said, when Julia told him, "that boy was a no-good source of endless irritation."

"I hope he won't do anything desperate."

"He won't. He'll go back to begging for a couple of days, and then he will return. He knows a good thing when he sees one. Besides, as far as I am concerned, he can hang himself."

Julia did not want a quarrel, but she was upset by this unexpected outburst. Pedro's name was no longer mentioned at La Bidouze. But—only Dorothy knew about this—Julia went to see the priest of the little village which belonged to her domain to discuss Pedro's problem at length. A few days later, she was discreetly informed that one of the foresters had found the boy in a cave, and that little Claire was bringing him his food. Julia told Michael that she had to leave for a couple of days to Digne, a nearby town, and, without Michael's knowledge, she put the boy in a Dominican College.

She told the abbot what little she knew of Pedro's background, wisely forgetting a few little details, and asked him to see to it that Pedro would get an excellent schooling.

"He is very unruly," she told the abbot, "and, though I do not wish to use the rod on him, I think you should be very strict. I will pay for all his expenses and I hope that this gift for the school will meet with your approval."

The abbot's eyes popped. The members of the de Corriero family had always been extremely generous to both College and Abbey, but this gift surpassed anything they had ever received.

"Madame can be assured that the boy will receive the best attention," he said.

"When the boy has finished his final exams, I hope that one of your good Fathers will bring him to me."

And so it was agreed. The gates of learning closed behind Pedro for a number of years.

* * *

The summer flew by on wings of love and the inhabitants of La Bidouze were surprised when they noticed one day that the swallows were gathering for their flight to the African shores.

"Already?"

"Yes, already. And it will soon be time to follow their example."

"To Africa?"

"No, silly . . . back to Paris."

Once back in Paris, not a night went by that Julia did not squirm in Michael's hot embraces. But the artist did not love Julia for her body alone. Granted, it was one of the most beautiful and desirable bodies in all of Paris because mother nature had spent a lot of time and thought when she created this gorgeous woman.

However, Michael also wanted her to share his knowledge and feelings. He decided to introduce his love to the world of the mind.

That winter they traveled through Italy. The summer was spent at La Bidouze, and the next winter was spent in sunny Spain.

Their repeated, prolonged absence from Paris had the happy result that, at least outwardly, the anger of the Count de Paliseul was subdued. He had sworn to himself that he would move heaven and earth, and if necessary go down to hell, to revenge himself upon Madame Pomegranate Flower.

The love affair between Maxim de Berny and Florentine was still going strong. Possibly both were a bit less passionate than they used to be, but they still saw one another regularly in the Rue Charles V. Possibly too regularly. Florentine was beginning to suffer. She lost weight, and she was beginning to get nervous. Her doctor diagnosed it as a lack of emotional involvement, and he suggested that Madame should seriously think about remarrying and having a few children as playmates for her growing son.

Five years went by without any serious mishaps. Five years of happiness as fate bestows only upon the lucky few. Both women had emptied the cup of earthly joys for three quarters. The last quarter was to be mixed with bitterness.

Julia was the first one to taste it.

During the season, back in Paris, she had been introduced to the Count de Paliseul. It came as a shock to her, but she quieted herself by insisting that he could not possibly have recognized her.

He did not. But, he had seen Dorothy without a mask, and he recognized her!

"Well, well, my dearest Madame Felicitas," he had said with a vicious snarl, "how the mighty are fallen! You are indeed in a beautiful home. But after having had one of your own, I doubt if you like the role of a common chambermaid."

Dorothy acted astonished, said that his Lordship was jesting, and Pierre, the majordomo, who had listened to the little scene, confirmed that Dorothy—like himself—had been in the service of Madame de Corriero for at least ten years.

De Paliseul, who was convinced that he did not make a mistake this time, put two and two together. Ten years! Those words stuck in his mind. But then, Madame de Corriero, the woman who was unapproachable, must be the lascivious Pomegranate Flower, the very same woman with whom he had spent a night of complete debauchery in the Rue Charles V!

Now his time of revenge was there! His evil tongue began to spread rumors, questioning the honor of the great Donna José de Cor-

202

riero. He began to imply—and in that he was not far from the truth—that the man who restored her castle might also restore her wild, lustful and carnal desires.

Julia, who did not have the slightest idea of what was going on, noticed soon that on various occasions she was being snubbed by her acquaintances. Women were positively spiteful, and certain men became more courteous than good manners allowed.

Michael, in his circles, had noticed a similar situation.

One night, when they were resting in bed Julia asked him, "Do you think that our love affair has become public knowledge?"

"I doubt it. Let's be honest, nine-tenths of your girl friends have an affair of one kind or another, and this would hardly be a reason for them to be so positively nasty towards you."

One evening, at a party thrown by one of Julia's best friends, they were to discover the reason.

The guests were breaking up in little clusters and Michael, who was sitting in a corner, happened to be next to the table where several members of the Club de Topinambours were discussing the women who paraded across the rooms. He could clearly hear everything that was said.

"Come on, de Paliseul," de Melreuse said, "don't try and make us believe that Madame de Corriero is this fantastically lascivious Pomegranate Flower you possessed five years ago. We know that story was a lie, and we have seen the old lady with whom you cavorted and whose twenty springs had left her ages ago. That whole ridiculous history in the Rue Charles V better be forgotten."

Michael blanched at the words "Pomegranate Flower" and "Rue Charles V." He was even more depressed when Julia walked by without noticing him, and de Paliseul continued, "That's her all right. And I have heard stories about her and an artist whom she meets regularly at the home of her sister, the widow Vaudrez."

And again, he smirked.

"Can't you, for once in your life, stop leering, and laugh like normal people," Maxim de Berny asked. De Paliseul was hewing home awfully close and he'd rather pick a fight than have this conversation continued.

But de Paliseul, who felt that his hour of triumph was near, could not be so easily persuaded to leave his favorite subject.

"Have none of you," de Paliseul continued, ignoring Maxim's remark, "noticed the striking resemblance between Madame de Corriero's chambermaid and Felicitas from the Rue Charles V?"

"What," de Melreuse exclaimed. "She is the lady with whom we caught you cavorting on that huge, silk and satin-covered bed?"

"She is the very same."

Exclamations of surprise, the wildest guesses, the vilest suppositions. The name of Julia de Corriero was on everybody's lips.

"And I would not be in the least surprised," de Paliseul continued, "if that painter fellow who is always at her sister's home, that Michael Lompret, is my lucky successor."

"Excuse me, sir," Michael said as he suddenly stood towering over the astonished Count

204

de Paliseul, "I just heard my name mentioned. I neither liked the way it was spoken, nor the matter with which it was connected, and I demand satisfaction!"

"Gentlemen, gentlemen!" Maxim de Berny tried his utmost to avoid the unavoidable.

"Sir, I beg you to stay out of this matter which only concerns me and the Count de Paliseul. I demand satisfaction, and I wish you to name time and place!"

"Nothing would be more pleasing to me, Mister Lompret, than to give you a taste of my sword. Tomorrow morning?"

That night, Michael did not go to the Rue Charles V, but to his own home. His heart was shattered. Doubt plagued his mind. Could it be true that de Paliseul had not been bragging? Could it be possible that the woman with whom he had lived in bliss and happiness for more than five years was in reality a common courtesan, as de Paliseul had said? Had the old General de Corriero been merely a father to her? His mind worked feverishly. The world was falling apart. Could it be that the Count Gaston Saski had been her one and only lover? After all, she was also known as the Viscountess Saniska! She had told him that she and her sister had been brought up by Aunt Briquart who was a Colonel's widow, and of simple means. Was Aunt Briquart truly a Colonel's widow, or was she an expert matchmaker who through certain liaisons had amassed a fortune. He now even began to doubt the innocent mother-son relationship between Julia and Pedro. After all, the miserable brat had tried to stick his little dagger in his

back. He had never told Julia that he had
guessed the truth, because it seemed painful
to his beloved. Painful! Bah! He had been
tricked for almost five years!

The next morning he went to Julia's home
on the boulevard St. Michel. He explained to
her that the party had given him a terrible
headache. He decided not to tell her about the
duel which would take place that morning. Under some pretext he left early, kissing her forehead tenderly. It was his farewell kiss.

"What's the matter, darling?" Julia asked
anxiously.

"Nothing, dear," he said, and turning to
Dorothy he asked her if she would come home
with him, because he had a present for Madame which he had forgotten to bring with him.

He handed her a precious jewel which he
had bought for Julia and asked her in passing,
as if it was nothing of importance, what was
behind that story of Dorothy's beautiful behind
which she had shown to the members of the
Club de Topinambours.

"Oh, that!" Dorothy laughed, and she told
him the whole story.

There was no doubt. His whole world had
fallen to pieces.

The next morning, his body was brought
into his studio and laid upon the bed where he
had tasted his first true happiness. His heart
had been pierced by de Paliseul who had been
very surprised by the fact that a man of Lompret's background defended himself so clumsily.

He was still alive when his friends put him
down upon the bed where he and Julia had
passed so many happy hours. Jonathan was

206

beside himself.   He did not even know Madame de Corriero's address.

And when Julia, informed by Florentine who had heard about the duel from Maxim, entered Michael's home, he had just breathed his last breath.

CHAPTER FIFTEEN

The sudden, premature death of Michael was a terrible blow for Julia. She had deeply loved him with every fiber of her being, and his parting almost killed her, too.

They had tried to hide the reason of the duel from her, but one of her vicious acquaintances—the moralist type that seems to grow like a cancer in every society—had anonymously written her all the sordid details, including the fact that Michael had not even defended himself. She alone, the vituperative letter concluded, had been responsible for her lover's death.

"He must have cursed me upon his deathbed," Julia said to Dorothy.

That, of course, had not been the case, but like all those who suffer, Julia found a certain comfort in wallowing in her guilt. Her health of body and mind suffered terribly; she did not even notice that her salon was almost empty on visiting days.

Dorothy and Florentine surrounded her with tender and loving care. The influence and the impeccable name of Count Maxim de Berny, who had come to the defense of Julia's honor wherever and whenever possible, made the rumors that spread through Paris slowly die down. De Paliseul was expelled from the Club de Topinambours because of behavior unworthy of a man of his standing, and finally, things returned to normal.

But the future before her showed nothing but grayness and loneliness. The months of suffering, illness, and pain had taken her youthful beauty, and the sadness of her heart showed in her eyes.

Julia retired completely from society and bestowed all the love of her entire being upon Claire.

"In another year, I'll take her out of the boarding school," she had said to her trusted maid, "and the girl will be a great comfort to me. She will ban the loneliness from my doorstep."

And indeed, Clair, who had grown up to a beautiful young woman, brought a ray of sunshine in Julia's heart. A few years went by and time, which heals all wounds, had its healing effect upon Julia. The smile returned to her lips and, though she often cried in silence, her beauty, more mature now, had returned. She was almost light-hearted when, two years after Michael's death, she decided to return to La Bidouze.

One afternoon when she was sitting before the window of one of the rooms overlooking the wide driveway toward the castle bridge, she noticed in the distance the white habit of a Dominican monk. Next to him walked a tall, dark young man. Coming closer, she noticed that the youngster was very good looking.

Dorothy announced the arrival of the venerable Father Martin and his pupil Don Pedro. The boy had received all the instructions which the Dominican College had to offer, and passed his exams with flying colors. The time had come, according to the abbot, that he was to be returned to his Mama, as Pedro called Julia.

It had not been easy for him, because his free gypsy nature had been difficult to subdue. The boy had known a life free of all conventions, his body had reached early maturity, and at times the severity of his teachers had seemed almost unbearable. But whenever his school-work had become too boring, or his teachers too severe, Pedro had recalled the lovely body and features of his beautiful "Mama," and told him-self, "Just wait till I am big and grown-up . . . till I am somebody . . . she has promised me . . . she would be the first one . . ."

Julia barely remembered her rash promise. But for Pedro it had been the one and only motivation to complete his difficult, hard studies for all those years. Julia was very glad to see her boy again, and enjoyed him calling her Mama. She thanked the good father for all his trouble and told him that she intended to keep the boy at La Bidouze till the University would open at the end of the summer. The monk left La Bidouze castle, laden with gifts.

Julia gave Pedro everything he had ever dreamed of. His own apartment in the castle, complete with living room, bedroom, study and library to which he alone had the key. From Paris she ordered everything a young man of standing needs, including beautiful books for his library. From her estates she gave him a good dog, a spirited horse, and a hunting rifle.

She had made up her mind to arrange a marriage between Claire and Pedro, to make them her heirs, and she was therefore extreme-ly surprised when, one evening, Pedro suddenly knelt in front of her and kissing her hands, reminded her shyly of that promise given a long, long time ago.

Julia deliberated. "I have," she thought to herself, "not done wrong when I promised him, after that punishment . . . And young or old, it's the only way for a woman to get things done . . . I will keep my word. I shall teach him what my poor Michael understood so well. That ecstasy only reaches its highest peaks when the body is guided by the combination of spirit and heart. The tender expression of love, and all that goes with it, depends upon the first woman a young man possesses. She alone has it in her power to make his love-life beautiful, or a never ending obscenity. But what am I thinking of? He is only expressing his gratitude. He does not really remember what I promised. But, if he does," she continued to herself, "I will guard and guide him to make sure that my little Claire will be happy with a perfect husband."

That night, when Dorothy helped her mistress prepare for bed, she told her maid that she wanted the nightgown with silk and lace, the one with the embroidered butterflies which Michael liked so much. Under it, she wore nothing.

When Dorothy had left, Julia opened the windows of her bedroom, and leaning upon the sill, she stared up at the pale moon and the sparkling stars.

She heard a sound behind her and suddenly she was caught by two strong, young arms. She turned around slowly, not in the least surprised to see Pedro.

"Mama," he stammered, barely able to suppress his excitement, "I love you!"

"I love you, too, my dear child. But we have time enough to say that to one another. This hour is hardly fitting to come to me."

"I love you, Mama," repeated the young man, "please tell me, what other hour could be more fitting for telling you this. Look at the beautiful moon and stars, listen to the rustling of the brook and the wind through the treetops. We are alone, completely alone. I was a poor little gypsy when you found me, starving in the bushes. You took me into your home and, I know, also into your heart. You have made me what I am today. But, if you extinguish the flame in my heart which has kept me going through all these years, I wish that you would have left me to die in those bushes. And you know . . . Mama . . . what flame I mean!"

Julia knew, but she wanted to hear it.

"Have you forgotten? You promised me! When you found me again after I had run away . . . you promised me severely, but when you talked to me, I knew that you loved me. Though I was a mere child then, I knew that I had deserved the punishment. But we were alone then, and there was nobody to laugh at me. And you took me on your lap, and you said things to me which I have never forgotten. I was naked, and your hands caressed me, giving me a feeling I had never felt before or since. You cradled me in your arms, Mama, without bothering about my nakedness. And it was then that you promised me, if I would behave and do as I was told, that once more I would feel your tender caresses; this time not the pain of punishment, but the secrets of love between man and woman. And that is what I beg of you now!"

"You have really never . . ."

"No! To have a woman in a boy's college . . . it's impossible."

"And other things . . ."

"Not that, either! The temptation was great,

212

but you had told me that I would become a miserable man without backbone if I were not capable of containing myself. And I have won! And tonight, dear Mama, tonight, please teach me—not how to love; that is not necessary, because my heart is brimming over. But how to express it. Please, Mama, teach me!"

Julia had always felt some regret that there was no chapter in her memory like that of Florentine and her little Cherub. Long, long ago it seemed when Florentine had told her about the young man she called Cherub. The boy had been a virgin and Florentine, who had been stranded with the boy in bad weather, had spent the night with him in a little town near Paris, named La Loupe. Nine months later, her sister had been delivered of her beautiful blond boy, a face which had made her husband, George Vaudrez, deliriously happy. George had gone to his reward, firmly believing that he had fathered a son.

Julia had often dreamed about a virginal Cherub and Pedro's pure words did not fall on deaf ears. She threw her arms around him and looked him deep in the eyes.

"That is your greatest desire?" she asked softly. "Are you very, very sure of that?"

"Oh yes, yes," Pedro exclaimed with a passion that knew no bounds.

"But my dearest child, do you realize that this heart, at whose gates you are pounding, died a long time ago?"

"Please, no . . . don't talk about that . . . I know . . . the other one . . . that you have lost him . . . I don't hate him any longer . . . and the fire of my love for you will make you forget him . . . forever! Please, I beg of you . . .

be mine. Be mine in the way you used to belong to him. Give me the same caresses . . . the same kisses . . . the same little cries of your love and lust . . . be mine . . . be mine!!!"

And Pedro kissed Julia, covering her with hot and passionate kisses.

"Come here . . ."

Julia squirmed out of his passionate embrace and pulled him toward the couch. Her heart was pounding. And though she did not exactly feel a deep love for the boy in that sense, her body had become excited for the first time in years. And she was afraid that she would destroy Pedro's trusting heart if she were too reserved.

"What do you want to do? Let's go into your bedroom!"

"No my child . . . here." And Julia reclined upon the pillows.

Pedro kissed her hair, her forehead, her hands. The child had become a man. A chaste man, but the blood in his veins had reached the boiling point. Julia knew that she could not postpone the crisis, lest it would end in a miserable failure of a premature ejaculation.

She motioned for him to undress himself and this time there was no punishment forthcoming. Pedro did not have to be asked twice. In no time he stood before Julia in all his glorious nakedness. Slowly she got up and walked toward him.

"You are beautiful," she said simply.

The silken negligée which covered her body was soon loosened by Pedro's feverish hands. Despite her sufferings, Julia's body was still as gorgeous as ever. Pedro had soon cupped one

214

of her breasts, covering it with wild, passionate kisses.

"Lie down here, close to me, my darling," Julia said. Passion had her in its grip now. "Put your chest upon my bosom, your lips against mine. Our breath should mix . . . let your tongue search for mine . . . put your hands around my hips and move them whenever your feelings tell you to do so . . . and here, here . . . deep inside me . . . let my love juices baptize you . . . flood me with those of your loins and let us enjoy together the rites of love!"

Pedro fumbled a little, but Julia was very understanding and she guided his throbbing spear toward her love grotto so that Pedro might enjoy his initiation, and he soon found his spear firmly imbedded in Julia's warm sheath. He had never been so happy. His entire nervous system vibrated from the tip of his toes to the top of his head, and he shook as if he had been hit by lightning.

Julia had stretched herself upon the wide bed, receiving Pedro with wide open thighs, taking his libation deep inside her belly. She had, without the boy's knowledge, played with her clitoris to augment her feelings. She wanted to be able to come at the same moment Pedro did.

The moment came quickly. For the first time in his life, a groan escaped Pedro's panting chest which announced the highest ecstasy of carnal pleasure. Because of its enormous intensity, it had almost been painful.

For a long time afterward he remained motionless in Julia's tender embrace. It seemed indescribably delicious to him to smell this undefined, intoxicating woman smell.

Usually the first experience is so weakening for a young man that he would want to fall asleep in the arms of his loved one. But here Julia drew the line. Reluctantly Pedro left her bed, not after having made her promise him to teach him all there was to know in the art of love. They kissed tenderly, and Pedro went to his own quarters.

During the three months they stayed at La Bidouze, Julia taught Pedro all she had learned about love. She also made it plain that in the final analysis, the goal of theory is the exercise of practice. She did not spoil the boy. On the contrary, she never failed to point out the disastrous results of licentiousness, intemperance and debauchery. She also warned him against the unnatural practices with members of his own sex which might cause him to waver between man and woman forever, and did not fail to tell him that a clean whore was, if the necessity truly arose, infinitely better than masturbation. The fantasies which he might create in his mind, while playing with himself, could never be approached by reality. She warned him that no fate was worse than the loneliness of the masturbator.

She combined the good care of a mother with those of a practiced teacher, and she succeeded in moving the strings of the boy's heart so that she was sure of a beautiful melody of love within it.

The day arrived that Pedro had to leave for the University. Madame de Corriero had a long, last talk with the boy who had wanted to become her lover, and whom she wanted to be her son. She talked to him about his future, warned him again against the dangers of excess and told him not to return till he had his degree.

Pedro protested lively, but he knew that the tiny body of his Mama hid a will of iron. As soon as she had said, "I want it," he knew that he could only obey.

Three years went by, and Pedro left the University with his doctorate. Madame de Corriero was at La Bidouze, and he counted the hours as the train crawled through the countryside. When he arrived late that night, leaping up the stairs, she did not answer his knocking, and the door to her bedroom was securely bolted. The next morning Julia explained to him, as tenderly as possible that the things which then were a necessity, would today have been positively nasty.

"Youth belongs to youth, my boy," she said. "I hope that you will always remember your Mama with love and tenderness. I have punished a little brat with the rod, I have made a man out of an adolescent. And that is the end of my role. I hope that you will save your love for one whose heart will beat your rhythm. The future, happiness and love . . . my dear son, there goes the very embodiment . . ." and she pointed at Claire who slowly walked toward them.

Pedro's protestations were very feeble indeed. Claire, who looked like a brilliant spring morning, made the beautiful image he held of Julia in his mind fade quickly.

And so it happened that Julia's wish came true. Her two foster children fell in love, and they needed no help from her. It did Julia's heart incredibly good when she saw the tender love bloom between these two beautiful young people.

Before she left La Bidouze, she was happy enough to see Pedro and Claire get married. She settled a large tract of land on their names, which included a marble quarry. With his mining degree Pedro would undoubtedly know how to extract the riches out of his mountains.

"I believe that I have made two people very happy," Madame de Corriero said to herself when she returned to Paris.

CHAPTER SIXTEEN

Florentine, too, was beginning to notice the raw edges of life.

She still had her affair with Maxim de Berny, but her health was suffering and it seemed as if she was getting worse by the week.

She was about to become thirty years old, and a crisis was quickly approaching.

Her doctor deemed it necessary to tell Julia about her sister's condition. A marriage was an absolute necessity.

"Unless she becomes a mother again, I cannot be responsible for what might happen. She is on the verge of a complete nervous breakdown."

"And do you believe that motherhood . . ."

"Maybe not the motherhood itself, but the attempts," the doctor said, "can be very useful."

Dorothy put it slightly differently when she remarked, "I have been trying to tell Madame Vaudrez that she needed a good fuck instead of that eternal muffdiving. One of these days she will go absolutely crazy."

The women decided to get Florentine out of Paris, if necessary by stealth, and to force her to break her relationship with Maxim de Berny. Florentine only stuck to him out of habit. She knew that the young man was whoring around in Paris, but she did not want to admit it.

One day, Julia simply took her sister on a long trip. They went to La Bidouze, and Florentine was enchanted with the old castle, the beautiful surroundings, and especially with Pedro and Claire who had joined them for a happy family reunion. The little Cherub, Florentine's son, was delighted with his big, strong uncle.

Meanwhile, Dorothy had informed de Berny about Florentine's situation and, in her mistress' name, she asked him to give Florentine her liberty. The Count willingly complied, and Florentine received a tender letter, asking her to give Maxim his freedom.

It seemed as if a load had fallen from Florentine's heart. Soon, the widow Vaudrez was her old, happy self again. The color had returned to her cheeks, and, though matured by ten years, she matched her sister in beauty.

The summer went by without any adventures worth noting. As a matter of fact, it had become somewhat monotonous. The sisters decided to spend a few weeks on the Riviera before they returned to Paris for the season.

High society from all over Europe gathered annually in St. Jean-de-Luz. The entire world seemed to have made this little town their rendezvous.

One day, the two ladies and the little Cherub were strolling through the town, when a voice suddenly exclaimed, "Madame Vaudrez!"

Florentine turned around, "Cherub! Darling!" Then she caught herself and blushed, "Your Highness!"

Gordon, Duke of Herisey, laughed. He looked at Florentine with tenderness in his eyes, and it was also obvious that he liked very much what he saw.

"What an extraordinary coincidence! Have you been here long?"

"Only a few days. Permit me to introduce my son, Cherub."

"*Our* son Cherub," Julia said mischievously.

"A beautiful name, Madame. He looks indeed, like a little angel!" And the Duke lifted the little boy high above his head, kissing him upon the forehead when he set him down gently.

"And where have you been all these years?" Florentine asked.

"In Japan. As you know, my mother always wanted me to travel for at least ten years before I decided to settle down. I am sure that she wanted to keep me out of the clutches of the Parisian ladies. But now I have had enough of traveling, and I am going to settle down as a good and solid citizen. I intend to live in Paris."

"I hope we shall see each other from time to time."

"Every day, unless you decide to throw me out!" Gordon smiled. "And now, my dearest lady, allow me to spoil little Gordon a little bit," he looked Florentine straight in the eyes.

"But, please, only a little bit. He is spoiled enough as it is, already."

"He must have inherited that from his father," the duke answered laughingly.

"And this?" Julia asked, ruffling her hands through the boy's golden curls.

"Those he has from his mother," Florentine said.

They continued their stroll, meeting Gordon de Herisey at the appointed place. The little boy was even more enthusiastic about this new "uncle" than he had been about young Pedro.

"Ladies," Gordon said, "I must take leave

for the moment. A very good friend of mine is in town, and I had promised to meet him at three o'clock. With your permission, I would be honored to present him to you."

"How amusing to met a good old friend after so many, many years," Julia said. "So this gentleman was your famous Cherub?"

"Yes," Florentine said, deep in thought.

"I wonder to whom he is going to introduce us."

"Probably to some Oriental he met during his travels."

That evening brought another surprise. It was not an Oriental to whom the sisters were introduced. It was no one else but Gaston, Count Saski.

He was no longer the dashing, young man of more than ten years ago. Time had weighed heavily upon his shoulders. His temples were gray, and deep lines furrowed his face. The deep-set, dark eyes betrayed that Gaston had suffered much.

For him, too, the times of love and laughter seemed to be over. During several stormy years, he had lost his wife, his children, and most of his fortune. Only Aunt Athena Saska had survived all misfortune, seemingly without bother. She still ate half a chicken daily, washing it down with a bottle of wine. Only her legs bothered her a little bit, and she had given up her habit of a daily hike through the forests.

Julia and Gaston looked at one another during dinner that night. Their emotions were mixed, but they were thinking along similar lines:

"He has suffered a lot . . ."

"She has cried often . . ." and . . . their

222

hands found one another under the table; their fingers intertwined.

"Can you forgive me?" he asked softly.

"I have forgotten," Julia answered simply.

*   *   *

Six months later, two travel coaches, loaded with luggage, were waiting in the courtyard of Charmettes castle.

Not far from them, two gentlemen were giving orders to the servants. One of them was Gordon, Duke de Herisey, husband of Madame Vaudrez since earlier that morning. The other was Count Gaston Saski who had just made Donna Julia de Corriero his wife in a simple ceremony.

And upstairs, on the balcony, two women stood, hand in hand. It seemed as if they were saying farewell.

They were no longer the two young girls, eager to fly out on their own, ages ago, from the home of their foster mother, Madame Briquart, the Colonel's wife. Time and experience had made them mature.

"Do you remember, Julia," Florentine was the first to speak, "how once we were so eager to fly toward our happiness?"

"Yes," Julia answered sadly, "but I will try to forget a lot."

"We are embarking upon an entirely new chapter in our lives, dearest."

"I know. But we have weathered the storms of our springtime, and we have survived the thunders of those storms. I am sure that we can handle the coming winds of fall. And I do not want to think, yet, of wintertime."

223

The two women cried, embracing each other.

"Let's go," Julia said, wiping away the tears. "Farewell to the past, good-bye tender youth, wild and passionate nights." She smiled sadly. "We are like suns, past noontime, rushing toward the evening."

"Evenings can be very beautiful," Florentine said. "We have a lot to live for. Our hearts may not be as passionate and wild as they once were, but there is still a lot of life left in them. And when our friends see us, arm in arm with our husbands, then they can surely see that the old proverb contains the wisdom of our ancestors,

"ONE ALWAYS RETURNS
TO HIS FIRST LOVE"

THE END